Hansda Sowvendra Shekhar is a doctor and the author of a collection of short stories, *The Adivasi Will Not Dance*, which was shortlisted for The Hindu Prize; and a novel, *The Mysterious Ailment of Rupi Baskey*, which won the Sahitya Akademi Yuva Puraskar and was also nominated for The Hindu Prize, the Crossword Book Award and the International Dublin Literary Award. His last published work was *Jwala Kumar and the Gift of Fire: Adventures in Champakbagh*, a novel for children. He also translates prose and poetry from Santhali and Hindi into English.

ALSO BY HANSDA SOWVENDRA SHEKHAR

The Adivasi Will Not Dance: Stories

The Mysterious Ailment of Rupi Baskey

Jwala Kumar and the Gift of Fire: Adventures in Champakbagh

My Father's Garden

HANSDA SOWVENDRA SHEKHAR

SPEAKING TIGER

SPEAKING TIGER PUBLISHING PVT. LTD
4381/4, Ansari Road, Daryaganj
New Delhi 110002

First published in hardback by Speaking Tiger 2019

ISBN: 978-93-88326-85-8
eISBN: 978-93-88326-23-0

10 9 8 7 6 5 4 3 2 1

Typeset in Arno Pro by SÜRYA, New Delhi
Printed at Sanat Printers, Kundli

With age everything turns viscous.
For hardening is a marker of age.
Knuckles, calluses, sores, scars; and the heart.
Madness is loose, fluid, it easily finds itself a home.
But not wisdom—maturity pickles, needs a container.
And so the viscosity of tree sap, the density of ageing madness.

—Sumana Roy,
'Tree Sap'

I want a boyfriend like a banyan tree. A man who's a forest unto himself, with conspiracies of birds, and secret blossoms, and shaded places; a matrix generous enough for the world.

And into this forest I will wander, a beloved of the world, and walk beneath the aegis of his boughs knowing that the same love that roots them raises me. I will become entangled.

—Sharanya Manivannan,
'Boyfriend Like a Banyan Tree'

LOVER

Samir slumps beside me as his arousal wanes. Getting him erect when he's this drunk is sometimes difficult, but I like doing it: massage his gym-toned shoulders, kiss the inside of his thighs, stroke and suck him. The first time we had sex, I had loved looking into his intoxicated eyes—the surprise, the hesitation, the escape in them. When he returned for more, I knew I had to keep him, whatever it took. Men are hard to find, and he was one to die for.

I lick his sweat-soaked chest with its day-old crop. I lick his tits.

'Maadarchod,' he grunts.

I lick his abdomen, stick my tongue into his navel. He jumps up. I laugh. He hates being touched there.

'Sudhrega nahin, laura ka baal!'

Later, when things changed, when I understood he wouldn't love me, but still craved him, he would still say this, and it would be as if nothing had changed: 'Sudhrega nahin.' No, I haven't reformed. Men are hard to keep. Dick-hair have a chance. And whores, bitches, cunts. Randi, kutiya, choot. He had many names for me when we fucked. Endearments that made me dizzy; I had learned to find pleasure in self-abasement.

'Neeche ja,' he says now, and I go straight to where I should have earlier. I pull down his foreskin, with its tiny mole on the right side, and I lick.

'Maa-dar-chood.'

It takes a while. But then he's ready again, and he holds my head still. 'Lie down. Lie down on your stomach.'

He folds my left leg at the knee and pins my right leg straight. He's so strong, this man who lifts and pumps iron, that I can't move even an inch.

'Saali, next time I want it shaved,' he commands, and begins. I feel like I might bleed and ejaculate at the same time. Is it pain? Pleasure? I don't know for sure. All I know is that at this moment he's all mine.

After he slumps over me, we remain motionless for a while, his naked skin against mine, in an embrace that I wish could last forever. He rises. I hold his arm.

'Don't go. Lie down with me for a few more seconds.'

He moves away, wipes his penis with an old newspaper, drinks a litre of water without stopping for breath, gets dressed and sprawls out on a chair in front of me. I watch him and hold out my hand.

He doesn't take it. 'This is too much hard work, boss,' he says.

That he calls me 'boss', the traditional way in which a junior addresses his senior in the medical college we both attend, gives me a chill. What am I doing, fucking a junior? I'm twenty-seven, a year older than him, already in my housemanship while he has yet to clear his degree exam. Also, he is a Mahato, from a different 'phylum'. I am an Adivasi.

And if having an 'intimate' Mahato friend were not bad enough, I was also letting him screw me.

It was I who started this relationship, drew him to me. A spark of shame races through me.

'Please wash yourself.' He covers my naked body with my chadar, the brute in him gone.

'Don't go.'

'I have to.'

'Why are you being so gentle now? You're so rough when we're doing it.'

'When we do it again, I'll be rough.'

'When?'

'Next time.'

He gets out of the chair and leaves, shutting the door behind him. I wait until I'm sure that he won't return, then I wrap a gamchha around me and head to the bathroom. I grip my penis. I see both of us sweaty and pumping. I smell his sweat, alcohol, cigarettes, oil. *Maa-dar-chood,* his voice rings in my head as I come.

~

After a year at university in Lucknow, I had arrived in Jamshedpur, to join medical college. My father had called me and said, 'Medical mein tumhara ho gaya hai. Your medical admission is through. Pack your bags and come home.' I said goodbye to Lucknow, collected my documents from the offices of the university, and reached Ghatsila. The very next day, family and friends accompanied me to Jamshedpur. It was quite sudden. And all I could understand was that I had been accepted into the medical college on a quota. At the college, I was whisked off to various offices and hostels so that the necessary formalities of admission could be completed. For the first time in my life, and certainly not the last, I understood the clout my father wielded, for all of his dissatisfaction at having been a failure at politics. Through my adolescence I had watched him withdraw into himself, become bitter and silent. But he had risen from the ashes for his son; it was an opportunity to flex some political muscle that still remained. Perhaps in securing my future, he was also trying to tell himself that he wasn't finished yet. Or so I hoped. I loved my father, I would let him shape my life. Because I knew that in a deep, fundamental way, I would never be the son he wanted.

Used to the relatively relaxed atmosphere of a degree college in Lucknow, medical college was a completely new experience for me. For the first couple of years there were regular classes which we were constantly dashing to attend; the syllabus was vast and immersive, and the examinations and tests constant. Yet, in those first years in Jamshedpur I felt liberated. Studies aside, there were the joys of a new place which were waiting to be explored. Slowly, I learned to quell the misgivings I had about my desires, about how my father, my parents, might judge me if they knew. I sought and found love, and love, of sorts, found me.

~

It began with Sunil Besra, in my first year. He was my classmate, just a couple of months older to me, and a Santhal like me. He played badminton and football, loved photography and junk food, read Osho, watched BBC, and had 'Veni Vidi Vici' printed on the front licence plate of his flaming red Pulsar 150. He made me read Tagore's stories to him because he loved to hear me read them aloud. My voice suited Tagore's prose, he'd say. We went to book fairs together and bonded over Rabindranath Tagore, Satyajit Ray and Rituparno Ghosh. He wanted me to teach him proper Santhali, for he was from the Santhal Pargana and I thought his Santhali was crass. Before each football match, he'd ask me to keep his glasses because, he said, 'I trust you.'

We were friends for a little over two years before we became lovers. The suddenness of it took my breath away. At school in Ghatsila, all of my grand love affairs had played out only in my mind. And Lucknow was an alien city which had to be negotiated with great care. It allowed me space to have crushes, to discover sparks, but not much more. In Jamshedpur, I was on familiar ground. At least that is what I thought.

It was one of those hot summer afternoons when nothing much seems to happen and the whole world sleeps only to escape the heat. Sunil and I were preparing to go out—I don't remember where, perhaps to an air-conditioned movie hall where we could spend a few hours in peace. I was lying on Sunil's cot, waiting for him to change his clothes. He walked in from the bathroom with a towel wrapped around his waist. But, instead of wriggling into his underwear underneath the towel, he held it open and flashed me. He then came up to me, held my face in his hands, and kissed me. His lips were like juicy orange slices. He played with my tongue, inserting his into my mouth, our teeth colliding. I guided his hands to my breasts and he squeezed them. I asked him to suck my tits, to bite them. He licked them first, *lap lap lap lap,* like a pussycat finishing a bowl of milk; then he bit them. And when I had squealed enough, he directed my hand to his penis.

'Give me a BJ,' he demanded.

Sunil's penis was like a porn star's, hard and

straight like a flashlight. When I took him, he sighed and combed his Dhoni-like nape-length hair back with his fingers.

'Should I?' he asked courteously before he came.

'Hmm ...' I signalled with my right hand.

Spent, he lay curled into himself. 'I'm sorry,' he said to me, head turned to the other side, not facing me. What was he sorry for? I didn't understand.

'It's okay,' I said, inching closer to him, touching his back. He shrugged me away.

'Go,' he said.

'I wanted to—'

'No,' he insisted, louder, his head still turned to the other side. He was quite sure he'd be the man in this. It didn't matter to me, I was happy.

But it wasn't just that. 'Please,' he said, 'Before someone sees us, leave.'

We always met in his room, and it never took long. I'd lent him my disc of Satyajit Ray's *Aranyer Din Ratri*. The memory game in the movie, which the characters play in the forest as a way of passing time, became foreplay for us.

'Sex,' he'd say.

'Sex, dick,' I'd respond.

'Sex, dick, semen.'

'Sex, dick, semen, erection.'

'Sex, dick, semen, erection, orgasm.'

That's as far as we'd get. Aroused, we'd undress and get down to business.

One night, he took a video of me giving him a blowjob.

I stopped when I realized. 'Fuck,' I said. 'What are you doing?'

He said softly, shrugging, 'Taking a video.'

I was shocked, but only for an instant. I trusted him. How else does one love?

I smiled. 'Do I look good?' He smirked and pushed my head down.

Even after Sunil and I became lovers, he made sure we were not seen together in public. He wouldn't even acknowledge me if I met him in class or in the corridors. Whenever he needed me, he'd give me a call. A missed call, usually at four in the morning—

he studied late into the wee hours—when nearly everyone in the hostel was asleep.

The song 'Childhood', from the soundtrack of the movie *Mandela* used to be my ringtone then. 4 a.m. My heartbeat would race as I peered into the display. Sunil.

If I took his call, the conversation would be just two words.

'Come.'

'Yes.'

I would apply Johnson's Baby Oil on the parts he'd soon touch, spray deodorant on my neck, chew two gums and, making sure there was no one in the corridors, creep stealthily past the rooms of doctors staying up late studying for the entrance exams to post-graduate courses until I reached his room on the second floor.

If we hadn't started fucking, I think Sunil and I would have remained friends. The sex changed all things. We no longer discussed Rituparno Ghosh's films. I no longer read him passages from the stories I wrote, from the books I purchased. We no longer exchanged DVDs, attend film festivals, raid roadside paav-bhaaji stalls, or talk to each other in chaste Santhali. I didn't really care.

Just days before he left the hostel, after I went down on him, he told me that he was planning to get married to a girl he'd chosen. She was a doctor, too, a beautiful Santhal woman with a broad smile.

'Please,' he begged, 'don't spoil my marriage.'

I was miserable after he left. I was angry. I didn't know why. I didn't know at whom. Maybe at Sunil. I threw things, broke things, I once splashed hot tea on myself. I cried, lying on my bed, all alone in my room, hoping that someone might hear, hoping that I might be able to talk with someone. But talking wasn't therapy.

Corex was. I couldn't sleep until I had gulped down a mouthful of Corex. I bought phial after phial, hoping all the time that Sunil would return to me. Pfizer should have awarded me a certificate for being their most loyal customer.

Corex made me sleep, but it made me even more miserable. It made me groggy, for one, and it gave me constipation, for that is one of the side effects of that syrup.

I was walking through my Corex haze, expecting Sunil to jump out of a corner and surprise me when I fell in love with Lucky, another of my classmates.

~

If ever there were fights in the college, mostly during annual festivals, with outsiders who came in drunk, Sunil and Lucky would be among the first to jump in. They'd grab the collars of the intruders and, without giving them a chance to explain, shower volleys of punches and kicks on them.

Lucky and I became close because of our shared love of travel. Jamshedpur was a new town for both of us and there was lots to explore. We would go on long bike rides and get drunk together in the resorts near the Subarnarekha River. He had a habit of chewing Rajnigandha and Tulsi, something I found quite uncouth, but which I later came to love.

'Why do you have to chew that?' I asked him.

'Have you seen a scooter being filled?'

'Yes.'

'What do they do?'

'Well, they fill it up with petrol. Then they put Mobil into it.'

'Rajnigandha is my petrol and Tulsi is my Mobil. My fuel and lubricant.'

Lucky was like a child; he collected Nagraj, Dhruv and Doga comics and constantly played games on the desktop computer he kept in his room. He loved dogs and had two at home, a purebred and a mongrel. He scandalized me by saying that he gave his dogs alcohol to drink. He danced with the hired dancers at our college festivals, flipping notes at them with his forefinger from a pile he held in his palm, matching them step to step as they gyrated to Bollywood item songs—'Babuji zara dheere chalo'—and crude Bhojpuri numbers—'Saiyanji dilwa maange le gamchha bichhai ke'. His dream woman, however, was Amrita Rao's character in *Vivah*, the ideal wife and daughter-in-law. He had a pencil sketch of hers pasted to a wall of his room. He always had several female friends at the same time, but only one special friend to whom he couriered stuffed hearts and teddy bears. When she came to town he arranged for a hotel room for the two of them.

Lucky had wide shoulders, a broad chest and bulky, muscular arms. He kept his back straight and his buns were taut and squeeze-worthy. He kept dumbbells under his bed, and a baseball bat for emergencies.

Smarting from the hurt that Sunil had inflicted upon me, I fell for him.

Our first night started out in a bar, a small dark place where people came to quickly get drunk and left. Samir—a little slimmer in those days, a regular gym-goer who rode a simple Hero Honda Splendor, and who was seriously in love with a woman classmate of his—had come with us, though I barely knew him then. Samir and Lucky were thick friends, even though Samir was junior to us.

To this day I don't know why I did it. Maybe I had sensed something in Lucky which told me that he was attracted to me. It is possible too that I was projecting my desire and my need on to him. Or it was simply the alcohol, which had made me uninhibited and bold. I slipped off my sandals and touched Lucky's crotch with my toes under the table. He spread his legs wide, nodding his head. Samir watched us in dazed amusement, innocent faced and wide-eyed.

At that time I was still the stern senior with him. 'Kya dekh rahe ho?' I asked.

He said with a deadpan expression, 'You are touching boss's dick.'

Lucky and I burst out laughing.

Afterwards, Samir went off to his room and I went to Lucky's. He took off his clothes and wrapped a towel around himself.

'Can I kiss you?' I asked.

'Yes,' he said.

We thrust our tongues into each other's mouths, enjoying each other's velvetiness.

'I want to fuck you,' he said.

I took my clothes off and oiled myself. He found Khaled's 'Didi' on his desktop and slipped on a condom.

Didi, didi, didi, didi didi zeen iddiwaah
Didi waah, didi, didi deedi ha zin didi

It became our fuck-song, matching the rhythm of our bodies.

Lucky and I would ride on his black Pulsar 150—with 'INSANE' written on its front number plate—to a dhaba outside town for beer and rum. On the way back, I'd fondle his chest and crotch, quickly removing my hands on seeing the headlights of an approaching vehicle. We would return to either his room or mine and do it wherever we could. On the bed, on the floor, against the wall. It was exciting at first, but I soon grew tired of it. Sex with Sunil had been tender at times, it certainly had a decorum to it. Sex with Lucky was wild. We would bite, scratch and hit each other.

Also, very soon after we began sleeping with each other, I started to get the feeling that Lucky was using me. That he was with me only for alcohol, and the endless eating out in dhabas and restaurants all over Jamshedpur.

'Daaru,' he'd demand, showing up at my room with only a towel wrapped around him.

If I refused, he would force his way in anyway. He would take off his towel as if he were doing a Chippendale act, remove my shirt, suck on my tits till we fucked. I would pay for his drinks.

This continued until, one night, I got fed up. He had come to my room demanding yet again that we go out drinking. I refused and, as was his habit, he took off his clothes thinking, obviously, that I would soon give in to him. Once he was naked, he started undressing me.

I held his hand and said, 'No, Lucky. Not tonight. I am not going anywhere with you.'

He put his clothes back on.

'Besra's gone,' he sneered. 'I'll go too. Let's see

if you find someone better.' Then he left, banging the door behind him.

~

There's something about a man who pumps iron and has rippling muscles and four-pack abs. It is taken for granted that he fucks well.

There were always people talking about beefy Samir in the hostel; about his conquests—women who worked at gents' beauty parlours; horny, full-bodied bhabhijis; nurses. Lucky had challenged me to find someone better and I decided it would be Samir—I'd show Lucky just how much better I'd done. Samir also had loutish charm, and I have always been attracted to the wrong kind of people.

Although I had barely spoken with Samir—except for a few social niceties—I did not hesitate to invite him to my room one evening, and he did not hesitate to accept the invitation. He wasn't the same Samir who'd seen me toeing Lucky's crotch. This Samir was a broken man. He'd failed to clear few of his exams and had been made to repeat a year; his girlfriend had left him for a senior; he had stopped going to the gym and had grown a paunch—though his body was still worth a second look—and he was drinking heavily.

He plopped himself on a chair. 'Hi boss,' he said. 'Lucky boss talks about you all the time. Why don't you go and see him?' Lucky now worked in a different hospital in a different part of the town. Samir spent all his evenings drinking with Lucky in his flat.

I ignored his question. 'You tell me,' I asked, 'which girl are you seeing these days?'

He smiled coyly. 'She's a nurse in Lucky boss's hospital.'

'How did you do it?'

'In the missionary position. Me on top.'

He'd misunderstood my question but ah! I could imagine.

A few days later, I invited him out for drinks. We were both high on cocktails of vodka and rum when we returned to my room. I hugged him and said, 'I want to kiss you,' my palms sweaty at propositioning a junior.

'What?' he asked, surprised.

I didn't repeat myself, I only grabbed his head, stuck my lips to his and sucked hard.

He sucked me in return and, when we were done, I told him, my heart beating hard at each word, 'I want your cock.'

'What?' This time he smiled, incredulous.

I started to pull down his fly.

'Wait, wait. Careful.' He unzipped his jeans himself. He wasn't wearing underwear. I discovered later that he never wore any, because according to him, that gave him a sense of freedom.

He was already hard, and sighed when I held his penis. But when I pushed the foreskin back, he said, 'No, no, boss. Not right, we are both ladka.'

'That's okay,' I said and slid out of my trousers and underwear. My palms were still sweaty and my stomach was tied up in knots, but now, I couldn't tell if that was because of nervousness or anticipation.

'Come,' I said, leading him by the hand to my narrow bed, but someone coughed in the corridor just then and frightened, he put on his jeans and ran away.

Only to return a few minutes later.

'I want to eat an ice-cream. It feels good after alcohol.'

I gave him a hundred rupees.

That evening, Lucky called me. Samir must have told him.

'Child abuse?' he asked.

'No,' I said, without a hint of shame or contrition. 'Consenting adults.'

To my surprise, Samir came to me the next morning. I woke up and there he was, sober and ready.

'You know boss, lubrication is very necessary,' he said, as if taking up a conversation we had left unfinished.

I undressed and bent on all fours. He undressed and slipped on a condom.

With his pumped-up chest and biceps, he looked

like a model for one of the protein supplements that bodybuilders eat. The only thing that spoilt the effect was his small paunch.

'Badhiya gaand hai,' he said, stroking and admiring my buttocks. 'Lie down.'

What? Lie down? He'd crush me. I preferred some liberty of movement.

'Lie down.' He was already on top of me, his lips on my nape.

'It's better—'

'Shut up and lie down.' He put his weight over me and pinned me down. 'There's no time.'

No one had ever used force with me. Samir did, and I found that I liked it. I offered myself to him, holding nothing back.

Samir was magical. He made me forget Sunil, and Lucky's taunts. I would return to the hostel from work, smelly from delivering babies in the labour room and the OT and, instead of taking a shower and changing into clean clothes, I would go to his room on the second floor and suck his dick.

At other times he would wait for me or pick me up from work and we would go out to drink. We came back late at night and slept in my room on the ground floor, fucking before sleeping, fucking after waking up in the morning. I wondered about the other women in his life but kept quiet about it.

Sometimes, though, I grew proprietorial. I was his first and only Facebook friend, but when, after a few months, spurred by a new-found confidence at having cleared his exams, he started adding more friends, the thought of sharing him made me so jealous I unfriended him. He had no idea till I told him, and he seemed unfazed. Facebook wasn't that important to him, nor was my friendship.

But when I told him why I had unfriended him on Facebook, he told me grandly, 'You can unfriend me, but I'll never leave you, jaanu.' He then took me in his arms and kissed my cheeks.

I had reason to be insecure for now he had a serious girlfriend now. A girl he called 'Moti'. She would usually call at midnight, many times when I would be with him. He would instantly turn into a gentleman. However long it took, he would patiently hear her day's complaints—a missed bus, a taxing training programme, indigestion—offering soothing words at intervals.

I knew he'd never tell me her real name. All I knew was that she lived in Santhal Pargana, a night's journey from Jamshedpur; she worked in a bank; and—like me—she too helped him with money and found his snoring annoying. I consoled myself with the thought that while Moti was waiting for her Samir, I was the one having sex with him.

They called Samir the Salman Khan of our medical college. He was such a huge fan of Salman that he had built his body like the star, walked, talked and danced like him, and, in the last year, had also started drinking like him.

The juniors idolized him, posing for photographs with him, their shirts off, flexing their biceps. These photos got enthusiastic comments on Facebook, praising his body and comparing him to his hero. Among the juniors he had one other nickname,

Doga, the buffed anti-hero character of Raj Comics. He waist had thickened from the drinking but his chest and biceps were still hard as rock.

I'm a couple of inches taller than Samir. One day, when we were walking together, he stared at me and said: 'You're taller than me!'

'Yes, I am,' I said proudly to tease him, straightening my back to look even taller.

As he dejectedly turned his eyes away from me, I smiled, put my arm into his, and said: 'Look, all of Sallu's heroines are taller than him. Aishwarya, Sushmita, Katrina, and that Sangeeta Bijli. Okay?'

He looked straight at me for a second or two, then smiled. 'You're right,' he said happily. 'After all, I am Salman.'

The front license plate of Samir's bike—a huge blue Pulsar 200—read YUVRAAJ, after the film starring Salman Khan. Except, the film's title had an extra V. I told him he should fix it.

He thought about it. 'I will need some money for it.'

'How much?'

'I think ... five-hundred will do.'

Even as I handed him the note, I knew he wouldn't correct the spelling. I could see that giving him money was almost the same as buying alcohol for Lucky, perhaps even worse, but I was past caring.

For Samir was all over me, on my body, inside my head. I tried at first to keep it physical, but he captured my mind. He would call me whenever he needed me, even when I was at work. He would come piss-drunk to my room and bang on the door, or bellow my name in his sexy voice, loud enough for the entire floor to hear. Secretly, I loved it all.

One day, he promised to take me to a beautiful place, with hills on both sides and a road running in-between, but the scoundrel that he was, Samir ended up taking me to Lucky's flat. Later, 'The Place' became our code-word for Lucky's flat: an idyllic road, bounded by hills,stretching endlessly into the horizon on which he would ride his bike, with me on the pillion, holding on to him. We sent

Lucky to buy alcohol—Blender's Pride for both of them and Smirnoff or White Mischief for me—and we had sex on Lucky's bed. We spread newspapers on it so that the sheet wouldn't be dirtied. When Lucky returned, he saw his bed nicely made up and balls of newspapers in his dustbin. Of course he understood.

'Saala, haraami log,' he told us.

Samir giggled shyly. I said, 'At least we didn't dirty your bed,' and laughed.

Samir and I were usually out of our hostel until 2 or 3 in the morning. He was an expert biker, even when drunk up to his eyeballs—he would ride at 60–70 kmph and dodge 10-wheeled trailers. I would just hold on to him, to my dear life. We went to risky places. Lonely spots by the Subarnarekha and the Kharkai rivers, places where we wouldn't go—or, rather, where he wouldn't take me—when sober. He would turn around and kiss me. I would unzip his fly and fondle him. Yet he would keep riding and I would keep fondling him. It was a miracle that we didn't have an accident, the police didn't catch us, and thugs didn't stop and rob us.

Samir had several friends. Sometimes he would bring a car and we would go out for night drives. He would drive. I would unzip him and suck him off. We sometimes got more adventurous and made out in public places. Outside the motorcycle parking of our hostel. In a corner outside the hostel mess, with the mess staff and our colleagues going in and out. On the terrace of our hostel.

On nights when I couldn't sleep after sex, but he would be snoring happily and naked in my bed, I would lock him from the outside to go to the common room of our hostel and talk with the others, smoke a cigarette, watch TV. I wondered if they knew what was going on between Samir and me. Then, on feeling sleepy, I would return to my room and find Samir lying spread-eagled on my bed, snoring deeply, his penis a small black bud. I would snuggle into whatever space he allowed me.

As always, he would get up at 6 a.m. I would, too, because my position on the bed was so precarious, even a slight touch would have woken me up. His eyes still closed, he would hug me from the back, tight, sticking his penis between my buttocks.

Eyes still closed, half-asleep, he would say to me groggily: 'Condom la.'

I would quickly get up, undress, throw him a Moods and lubricate.

Once he finished, he would pee out of my window, drink an entire bottle of water, dress up, and leave.

I couldn't concentrate on anything, and worried that I'd end up neglecting myself and my work. Samir lied to me, made up stories about himself and the women he'd had. He told me he also dealt in arms, that he knew the Naxalites and the coal mafias of Dhanbad, that the scar he had on his shoulder was where a goonda had touched him with a burning cigarette, and that he had beaten that goonda to a pulp. He later told me that the scar was self-inflicted, because he wanted to have a scar like Salman Khan had. With each story I desired him even more.

And I knew, or tried to convince myself, that there was some good in him.

First, Samir got up at 6 a.m. Sharp. This was perhaps a remnant from his serious body-building days. Even if he hit the sack at 2 or 3 a.m., he would be up at 6 a.m., fresh as a flower.

Second, Samir was a typical Virgo—very fastidious with how he carried himself and how he kept his room. His life would be in a turmoil, but not the hair on his head. If Salman Khan took his hair seriously, so did Samir. Salman straightened his hair (for *London Dreams* and *Wanted*); Samir did the same. In *Dabangg,* Salman returned to keeping normal, combed hair; Samir followed suit. If I pulled at his hair during sex, he would get angry. Afterwards, the first thing he would do was fix his hair. He would throw cigarette stubs and his clothes all over my room, but kept his own room very tidy. There would be cigarette holes on his bed-sheet, but it would be spread neatly. If he fucked me on his bed, he would make sure to straighten out the sheet even as I was lying upon it. He looked smashing in jeans and T-shirt but, being a doctor, he believed in wearing mostly formal clothing. Sharply tailored, ironed shirts and trousers; shiny, polished leather shoes; a big wristwatch; the Ray-Ban sunglasses that I had gifted him on his birthday.

Third, Samir loved children, and they loved his muscles. During paediatrics duty, I once heard him singing a Salman Khan song to a child with Down Syndrome because he wanted to see if children with Down Syndrome really liked music. Of course, the child was laughing in delight. And one day, we were hosted by a ward-boy from our hospital. He had a teenage daughter—who served us tea and arrowroot biscuits—and a son aged seven or eight. While I quite unthinkingly dipped my biscuits in the tea and gulped them down, Samir had the presence of mind to call the small boy to him, ask him his name, which school and class he was studying in, and offer him all his biscuits. The boy laughed happily and took all of them.

Fourth, Samir was actually caring. During a Saraswati Puja at our college, he remembered to bring a box of prasad for me. I wasn't expecting it at all. I was not even at the puja. But Samir returned from the puja on his Yuvraaj with two boxes of prasad placed on his lap, one for himself and the other one for me.

'Aap ke liye,' he said as he extended a box towards me.

I had every logic to believe Samir was ordinary, just like all of us. But he somehow seemed special. The things he did, the things he said, the way he carried himself. The more I tried to understand him, the more I started losing myself to him.

I would wait for him night after night, for the roar of his bike, up until one or two in the night when he finally knocked.

'I'm very tired today.' He came in smelling of alcohol one night and lay prone on my bed.

'I'll massage you.'

He stripped and I poured Johnson's Baby Oil all over his back. I started with his thick, burly shoulders, huge enough to hold up the world. Soon, once I'd aroused him enough, he was upon me, wrapping his beefy arms around me.

I moved down his back, the moles and scars I knew so well. I could have told him apart from all the men in Jharkhand by those moles alone.

'Lower,' he mumbled.

I parted his buttocks, rubbed oil in the softness of his crack. His buttocks had gooseflesh. Dot dot dot dot... I poked each, counting them. I parted his buttocks and licked. He rose on all fours, exposing himself.

'You look beautiful,' he told me tenderly after we'd finished.

I smiled.

'Boss,' he said.

'Why do you call me that?' I asked.

'Okay, sorry,' he said. 'Jaan.'

'Yes?'

'I need some money.'

'How much?'

'Two thousand.'

'Two thousand?' I turned towards him. 'I gave you that much two days back. What do you want this for?'

'I've borrowed some money from a friend. I need to return it.'

'Okay. Take my card.'

When he returned after fifteen minutes, I said to him, 'You always talk about your friends. You never take me to meet them.'

'Why? Why do you want to see my friends?'

'Why shouldn't I?' I reasoned. 'I've got every right to meet whoever you meet.'

'They're not good people,' he said. 'They're gangsters, they've got guns.'

'And they'll shoot me, right?'

'You don't understand, jaanu.' He came and sat by my side, stroking my naked back. 'I can't let you meet them. It won't be right.'

'Forget me then.' I turned over to the other side.

'Jaan.' He shook me.

'No.'

'Fine, I'll take you.'

'Today.'

'Today?'

'Yes, today.'

'Okay,' and after a pause, 'today.'

I waited the whole day. He didn't show up. I called him.

11.30 p.m. 'Some of my friends have been caught drinking on the road. I'm at the thana to get them released.'

12 midnight. 'I'm arranging money for their bail.'

12.45 a.m. 'I'm talking to the bada-babu.'

1.15 a.m. No answer

1.25 a.m. This number is busy. Please try later.

1.30 a.m. This number is switched off.

1.45 a.m. This number is switched off.

2 a.m. This number is switched off.

He arrived in the morning, sober, bathed, chewing Rajnigandha-Tulsi.

'Sorry, jaanu.'

'Not this way. I'll meet your friends.'

'Look, it's not—'

'Either you take me or you leave.'

'Your duty?'

'I'm not going to work today. I'm going with you.'

He stood at the door, speechless, while I pretended to be busy.

'Tum samajhti nahi hai, pagli.'

Yes, the foolish girl did not understand. She didn't want to. 'Hum ko nahi samajhna hai,' I said sternly.

'Okay,' he said meekly, and then he told me the rules. 'There, you are not to do what you do with me here.'

'What is that?'

'The place where we're going, the people there see me as a leader. I'm respected there. I have an image to maintain. And you have to give me some money.'

'Okay.'

The place was a dam resort on the Subarnarekha some thirty kilometres outside town. His friends, I saw, were from the working class. There was Samir's friend from school, a transporter who was a Karmakar; and four Adivasis who worked for the transporter. We were later joined by a few students from a local engineering college—all Samir's friends and fans from the gym—and two of our juniors from the medical college. Only the transporter called Samir by his name, everyone else called him 'boss'.

I wondered what Samir was trying to do. Laying the field for a possible political career he so often boasted to me about? And what kind of respect was it if it came from a bunch of friends and yes-men? Everything about him was so mindboggling.

The juniors were surprised to see me. They couldn't believe I had come with Samir because I was seen as posh, reserved, and—well—delicate.

'Aap yahaan?' they asked. 'With Samir boss?'

I couldn't explain my presence.

'Yes, boss wanted to see this dam,' Samir said, though they didn't seem entirely convinced.

Alcohol saved the day. After they started drinking, my presence was no longer an issue. I didn't drink; I wanted to stay in my senses, to observe, to take notes. They talked about the transport business, big money, women, other men's wives, the whores of Jamshedpur. Samir and the transporter were the most boisterous of all, flaunting their political reach, their contacts with the police top brass. I was treated with respect because I was Samir's guest. I was given the best chair to sit on; a separate plate to have the chicken chakhna from while they attacked the common platter; sealed Bisleri bottles while they drank from jugs. What am I doing here? I wondered about my place in that unlikely company, my situation, the pains I was taking to be with Samir.

Drunk, Samir was his usual boisterous self. 'Haraamkhor! I eat zinda maans!'

Sunil wasn't like this. There was a silent humility to Sunil, a determination to reach his goal without needing to talk about it or flaunting his contacts. Samir was the opposite. I had heard him answering evasively to phone calls from his family. His family perhaps knew what all he was up to. Drinking, spending himself. How did they take to all that?

I wanted to know all about Samir. Now that I had met his friends, I wanted to meet his family. If only getting him to take me to see his family were easy. Getting to his friends had taken me two days of tantrums and a decent sum of money.

I had heard Samir mumble in his sleep, an insecure soul inside a cocky body, living in the present, planning his survival second by second. He abused people in his dreams. Which people were these; I couldn't understand their names. Maadarchod, bhenchod, gaandu ... He spoke such words in his dreams. Samir never slept peacefully. Sometimes he slept with his eyes open; sometimes he turned to one side, his body held up on his elbow; sometimes on all fours after I rimmed him; sometimes with me sitting on top of him, pumping while he just snored.

I stuck to Samir's instructions and kept my hands off him among his friends. But when we sat down to dinner at a dhaba after drinks, all of them made Samir and I sit separately on one side of the table while they sat on the other side. Samir brought his chair close to mine. Smoking a Navy Cut, he placed his arm around me and squeezed my shoulder. I wondered if others were watching. Yes, they were, but they were busy with their backslapping and laughs. I removed his hand from my shoulder, putting on a straight face. Someone was playing a Sadri folk tune on a mobile phone.

> *Iskool kay tame pay, aana gori dame pay*
> Fair girl, bunk your school and meet me at the dam

Samir raised his bodybuilder's arms and waved them above his head. He knew I loved watching him dance.

'What is that, boss?' one of our juniors asked.

'I am trying to do the chhau.' He grinned. 'A very famous dance they perform in Saraikela district. I'm doing it for boss.' He put his arm around me again.

'Looks like Salman's dance to me,' the junior quipped.

'Arrey, why not?' Samir said animatedly. 'I'm Salman. That *Tere Naam* is the story of my life.'

Tere Naam. This was the seventieth time I was hearing Samir announce that the story of the film paralleled that of his life. I made a face.

'And here is my Katrina,' he whispered into my ear and kissed it. 'I hope you are not bored.'

'No.' I shook my head.

'How are you feeling?'

'Very happy.'

'You like my friends?'

'Yeah, but they're not dangerous at all.'

'You've seen nothing.' He grinned. 'That's why I was avoiding bringing you here.'

'I'd have come anyway.'

'Why?'

'Because I love to meet people.'

'Yeah?' he smiled.

'Yeah.'

He lowered his head and kissed my neck.

Later, when I went to wash my hands, he chivalrously accompanied me to the bathroom and kissed me on my cheek. I couldn't tell if anyone noticed or not. Actually, I didn't care. I needed

Samir, I had him, he was kissing me in full view of his friends. What else did I need?

'Boss,' Samir told me one night, 'I want to do something with my life. I want to become a good man.'

'You will,' I ran my fingers through his hair, one of those rare occasions when I could do it, since he was in that contemplative mood, so vulnerable, so unlike Samir, the Samir the world saw.

'I am a very bad man. I don't like myself.'

'No, you're not bad. I wouldn't have liked you then.'

He sat up on his elbow and touched my face. Then he lay down. I placed my head on his chest. He took my Nokia and clicked a picture of us together. Then he undressed and I began massaging him.

'Jaan, will you keep on massaging me like this?' he asked.

'Marry me,' I said, 'and I'll live with you.'

'Only if you were really a woman,' he said tenderly, as if he meant it.

At about midnight, as usual, his mobile rang. He grabbed his trousers and, covering his crotch, rushed off into to a corner.

'Moti!' he slurred into the phone, trying to sound sober. 'Had your dinner, darling?'

I covered myself with the blanket and watched him fumble with his clothes, as if the girl he was talking to would jump out of the phone and catch him red-handed.

'Not slept yet? Why, love? ... Waiting for my call? ... Sorry, jaan, very sorry ... I was busy ... Had your medicines? ... Go to sleep, you have work in the morning ... I'll come to you soon, very soon.'

He was upset after the call. I sucked him: a hurt, half-hearted blowjob. I massaged his back as he snored. I tried to check his call list but his phone was password protected. I picked up his wallet to go through it and found the receipt of the watch that Moti gifted him on his birthday, the same year I had gifted him the Ray-Ban. It was a Timex which he wore at all times, even in bed. But what hurt was to see both the Timex and Ray-Ban receipts tucked together.

But what ultimately shattered me was that Samir never kissed me. Never. He would kiss my neck, my back, my cheeks, my nipples, my abdomen, that place near my lips, even my buttocks, but not my lips. I longed to be kissed on the lips. Every time I would ask him, 'Why don't you kiss me?' he would say, 'A kiss is for someone special.'

~

Jamshedpur is connected to my hometown of Ghatsila by train, a distance of about forty kilometres. Among the regulars on the train is a group of hijras. They walk up and down the compartments, asking for money from the passengers, sometimes quietly, sharply clapping their hands sometimes, making a scene. They know which passengers are regulars and generally leave them alone.

I used to be a regular passenger on that route. The train would be crowded most of the time so I would not get a seat. I would be squeezed in the aisles or standing near the doors. The hijras would make their way through the coach, asking for money. They would just pass me by even though I would be standing right in their way.

While I was doing my housemanship in the hospital, my father called me to say that I should appear for the Department of Health exams. If I passed, I would become a government doctor. My father's word was command, at home, and in my life. I sat for the exams, and passed. It would take some time for my place of posting to be confirmed and I was suddenly at a loose end.

Sex with Samir was just that, sex. But I wanted more. I wanted him to be mine, I wanted him to kiss me, to say that he loved me, and only me. None of these would ever come to pass.

I made a hard decision: I resolved to leave Jamshedpur immediately and go to Ghatsila, to my parents' house. When the notification of my posting arrived, I would travel from there. In a very significant way, my father had precipitated one more turning point in my life.

Samir saw me off at the railway station on the day I left, sweet and caring in that masculine way that had always swept me off my feet. That morning, I had eaten him and afterwards, asked him for one farewell kiss on the lips. He had refused. Of course he said would stay in touch. And I knew it was a lie.

There was a V-front brief which he had left behind in my room one night after having sex with me. It never struck me to ask him why he had been wearing it that day. Perhaps he wanted to give me something to remember him by, because he was done with me. I brought it along.

In the train, the hijras again passed by my side. The train wasn't crowded that day, and I had found a seat by a window, but the hijras still did not seek money from me.

That day, I thought about their lives, these hijras. I wondered if they were in relationships and if their relationships were permanent, complete. I wondered if they too lived with a piece of cloth that smelt of the sweat and semen of a lover who couldn't be, wouldn't be, theirs.

I got a posting in a hospital in Pakur and moved there. I tried to keep in touch with Samir but he remained elusive. I stalked him on Facebook, saw him making friends, sent him messages, and then, one day, he blocked me. I gave up, and for several years, we did not speak at all. There was no phone call, no text, nothing. I got information about him from others, and, all the while, I yearned to hear his voice, to smell his smell. Of course I knew that not even a trace of our relationship remained, but a tiny hope lived inside me. It grew and grew and became unbearable until, one evening, I snapped under the weight of that monstrous hope. There were a lot of things going on in my mind and I was feeling so defeated I ran a knife over my wrist.

I slept through the pain, hoping never to wake up again, but I woke up the next morning, saw a blob of congealed blood near my bed, and I realized how stupid I had been. I returned home, to my parents.

During that period of recovery, I decided I had to go meet Samir. I did not know what to expect from the meeting. I did not even know what I wanted from him exactly. I only went with some faith in my heart that I would be able to meet him. I went to him with all my wounds; some open, some healing.

He was shocked, as I had expected him to be. He freaked out. 'Kya banjhi-banjhi kaam karte rahte hain aap? Kaahe kiye aisa?' he screamed at me. Why did I do it? What could I tell him? That I was happy I could shock him? That it was my revenge for seven years of anxious, sleepless nights? None of it was true, some of it was true.

He regained control of himself soon enough. This wasn't the Samir I had left behind, a man with loutish charm, obsessed with his hair. This Samir was formal, serious, grown up. He had a job now, his hair was cut short and combed so neatly that not one strand stood out. A formal-looking ballpoint pen was clipped to the pocket of his formal shirt, the type of shirt doctors are expected to wear. Instead of jeans, he had on a perfectly stitched pair of trousers. To me, Samir had always been bright and special. But today, I could see him shining with confidence. Even the scare that I must have given him did not dim his shine even a bit.

'Why did you do this?'

'Because I was very sad and had no other way,' I said. I was not calm inside, but made sure to keep the despair out of my voice.

'Will hurting yourself give you a way?' he asked, calmly.

I hate thinking about it this way, but I was secretly and intensely envious of him. How could he be at peace? I was envious of his calmness and his happiness. I was suffering away from him, how could he be happy away from me? Had he found someone? Was he seeing someone? Was it Moti, was she really enough? I was lonely, why wasn't he? Did he have a platinum spoon in his mouth? If I was suffering, why wasn't he? Or was he not happy but only pretending to be? I did not seriously believe I had mattered so much to him that he would be unhappy without me, but life made me unhappy, every hour of living made me unhappy, this was the condition of life, and if this was so, why wasn't everyone drowning in misery, why wasn't he?

And he had said he did not like himself.

Samir was, is, and will remain a conundrum however hard I try to understand him, like that Salman Khan character in *Kick* who says, 'Main dil mein aata hoon, samajh mein nahin.'

It was a very brief meeting which neither of us wanted to extend. I returned home. I had never imagined that one day I would receive counselling from Samir but, on my way back, after he had told me that I was a good person, that I was special, I found myself happy—though the feeling lasted only a couple of hours. I realized that I had made a lifeboat of just two kind words from Samir. It was a compromise, and a sorry one. For what I really wanted was him. I wanted Samir, entire. Not his words but him. His body, his breath, his entire being. I wanted a completion that I would find nowhere, with no one. I was meant to sink, I was sinking.

As I made my way back to Pakur, I found myself crying on the train. I was tortured by my inability to tell my parents about my choices, by the thought of the pain and disappointment I would cause them if I spoke the truth, by my inability to accept what I did not want to accept. All of it, everything that I felt and was yet to feel, was flowing out of my eyes. I must have known a storm was coming, because I had worn dark glasses that morning. And I took care to see that my face did not contort. I made no sound.

The group of hijras came into the coach I was in. They came near my seat but did not ask me for money. Maybe they still remembered that I was a regular passenger. Maybe they recognized me despite the shades on my eyes. Something came to my mind then: I took out my wallet and handed over the first currency note I could grab. I realized that it was a hundred-rupee note only when a hijra began counting change. They held ninety rupees before me. Ten rupees was what they took from people. I looked at the money but did not look up, afraid that they might see me crying.

'No, keep it all,' I said.

'Should I?'

'Yes.'

The hijra was perhaps surprised, but they took the note.

At a connecting station, I was standing near an Uber pick-up point. A driver passed me by lugging two huge bags. A young woman followed him. She had a bag slung from her shoulder and was dragging a large suitcase with wheels. Following that woman was a couple: a man and a woman, frail with age, walking slowly, cautiously. The man was holding the arm of the woman and it was hard to tell who was supporting whom. It was a reality I felt I could only aspire to, growing old with someone whom I could trust. Who would offer me an arm when I was sixty? Whom would I offer mine? Standing beside that Uber pick-up point I felt like bawling my heart out. My parents' faces flashed in my mind, Samir's face flashed in my mind.

Time passes and things get better; wounds heal and some things are forgotten. After four months, I had some official work in Jamshedpur, after which I was going back home. I boarded the train. Once again, I couldn't find a vacant seat so I stood near a door. The same group of hijras passed me, asking people for money. I immediately took out my wallet, though they hadn't asked me for money, and handed over a ten-rupee note to the hijra standing close to me. It was the same hijra I had given the hundred-rupee note to. I wasn't crying this time. I wasn't wearing shades. I was as happy and peaceful as I could reasonably be.

The hijra took the note from me and asked, 'Poora hai?'

I think I knew what that question meant. But I did not know what to say.

They waved their hand vertically, twice, before my body, and asked again, 'Sab poora hai? Complete hai? Kuch missing toh nahin hai?'

'Na, na, kuch missing nahin hai. Sab complete hai,' I said with a start. 'All okay. Nothing missing,' I added in English, as if that would convince her.

With great tenderness on her face, they placed a hand on my head, touched my cheek and walked away. I stood there wondering if everything was really complete, if I was whole.

FRIEND

I was home in Ghatsila. My father was working in his garden, like he always did, though he appeared calmer. But every time I saw him, I would feel a quiet panic. I lacked the vocabulary, the courage and the cruelty I needed to tell him that I was not the son he expected me to be. And if I did, would he understand? Would my mother? My double life haunted every hour of my life. I couldn't stop thinking of Samir. Where was he now? What was he doing? Did he love me still? Did he love me ever, at all?

Then the official notification arrived, instructing me to report for duty at the Sadar hospital of Pakur, a district in the eastern corner of Jharkhand. Pakur was far from Ghatsila, but equally distant from

Jamshedpur, from Samir, and I was happy. I felt the need to escape the drama in my life, to be alone, to gather myself together once more. Nothing worked, eventually. The grief grew too much to bear. I cut my wrist and returned to the shelter of my father's house, but this is not that story.

~

This was my first posting, the first job of my life, and my parents travelled with me to Pakur. We found a small room in a three-storeyed building near the railway station where I would stay for a couple of months until I found a house to rent. Once the formalities of the official joining of duty were completed, my parents left.

Work at the hospital was not very hectic. Though the only government hospital for miles around, it had, for some reason, been built away from the town centre and patients found it difficult to travel all the way there. Most of those who could afford doctors' fees would go to the private clinics in town and the patients we got were mostly accident victims or people injured in maar-peet clashes; the police were required by law to bring them to the government hospital first. We were often forced to refer the serious cases to hospitals either in Malda or Rampurhat in nearby West Bengal because the hospital didn't even have a functional X-ray machine.

At the time when we were completing the formalities of my joining, the head clerk of the hospital, whom everyone knew as Bada Babu, had been effusively helpful. It is in my father's nature to make friends easily, especially when he needs something done. He seemed to have worked his magic on Bada Babu, too. My joining was smooth and hassle-free.

One day, soon after I began work, I was in Bada Babu's office, sitting across his table to clear up some doubts about my employment contract. He patiently answered me and then, out of the blue, he leaned his portly frame forward and said, 'You know Sir, your father is a great man.'

I was taken aback. They had met only a couple of times, what had my father said to impress Bada Babu so much? 'Achcha?' was all I could manage.

'Ji,' said Bada Babu. 'I found out about him, and your family. Such a great man.'

I smiled self-consciously.

Bada Babu wouldn't stop. 'And you know Sir, before he left, he requested me to look out for you and help you.'

I did need some help at that time. The room in the building near the railway station was enough for me, and the area clean, but the room was small and hot in the summer months, and the neighbourhood terribly noisy, with trains clattering past at all hours of the day. So I told Bada Babu that.

He was shocked. 'Arrey Sir, you are staying there? That's no place for our daktar babu. Give me a few days and I will find you a house.'

And thus began an unlikely friendship in that small town, one that began with jollity and ended with disillusionment.

True to his promise, Bada Babu called me up

within the week. 'Sir, kahan hain aap? If you have some time after duty, I will show you a house.'

That evening, Bada Babu took me on his motorcycle to Madhyapara, a locality that was, as its name suggested, literally in the middle of Pakur. We reached a two-storeyed house belonging to a Brahmin family. The family welcomed Bada Babu with warmth and a degree of deference. After serving us tea and biscuits, he took us to the ground-floor—a suite that comprised two bedrooms, a hall and a kitchen.

Bada Babu told my would-be landlord, 'Mishra Ji, yeh hamare hospital mein daktar babu hain. Take care of him.'

Mishra Ji seemed delighted to have a doctor as a tenant. But the way in which he had greeted Bada Babu left me with little doubt that there wasn't much Mishra Ji wouldn't do for Bada Babu.

And thus I found the house which would become my home in Pakur.

It was comfortable and airy, but bare. I bought a cot, a mosquito net, a table and a chair. All my clothes stayed in my suitcase and backpacks. The kitchen had only a concrete platform on which I kept everything: a portable gas cylinder with an attached burner, the few utensils I needed to make tea and boil eggs and Maggi, packets of sugar and salt—the bare essentials. I also bought myself a motorcycle. I ate all my meals outside, in small restaurants and at roadside thelas. For a while I dearly missed my room on the top floor of the Ghatsila house, my many bookshelves, the sagwan outside the window and my father's garden spread out underneath the verandah. Then once I realized missing home was futile, I stopped.

Like most places in Jharkhand, which only became a separate state about two decades ago, Pakur is a village that went to sleep one night and woke up the next morning to find that it had become a town and the headquarters of a district. Not enough time had passed for it to acknowledge this change, for it to expand itself and become a proper town, let alone a planned city. Madhyapara too reflected this.

The house I lived in opened directly into a narrow alley. These alleys, which must have once been rough footpaths for pedestrians, crisscrossed the neighbourhood and had been cemented over by the Public Works Department into concrete streets. Looking out of my window, I could see many houses which seemed like they had been transplanted from the Bengal of the sixties: built of mud, double-storeyed but squat, their walls punctured by small windows with vertical iron bars in them, topped by sloping roofs and awnings made of tin. These wattle-and-daub houses jostled with modern concrete structures. But whether built out of concrete or mud, the doors of all houses opened directly on to the PWD roads. At all hours of the day, housewives in nighties would sit outside on the road, chopping vegetables, cleaning rice, combing their hair, quarrelling or gossiping. The municipal water pipes were laid beside these PWD roads with taps at regular intervals. Young girls and old women would wash clothes and dishes at some of these taps when the municipality supplied water.

Men would squat with buckets and mugs on the roadsides, morning and evening, for baths. And, at all times, I could see long rows of containers—steel and plastic buckets, jerrycans—lined up before the taps, waiting for their turn. Shrill fights would break out now and then when someone came to check and found that her vessel had been moved. It was the job of the children to keep a watch on the containers, and in between running off home to report, they would chase each other and play games. And snooty goats, reared especially for Eid—lovingly bathed by their owners in summer and protected from the chill of winter by warm sweaters—would live out their entire lives in the middle of these roads, too proud to move even after motorbike horns had blasted a thousand decibels against their ears.

After the madness of medical college, regular routine was what I sought, and regular routine was what I found. I would ride my bike to hospital, stopping on the way for meals—greasy luchis and aloo for breakfast, and regular restaurant fare for lunch and dinner. At work, too, things were routine—minor cuts and bruises, diarrhoea epidemics, government-directed vaccination and anti-polio drives to be implemented and reports prepared and sent.

I would occasionally meet Bada Babu. He would greet me. 'Namaste Daktar Babu. Hope Mishra isn't giving you trouble?'

'Oh no, not at all, everything is fine.'

Or, at the beginning of March, when all of us had to file our income returns, he would come to the doctors and other administrative officers on his own, saying, 'Sir, aap ka tax ban raha hai. To save it, you invest in this LIC bond.'

And we would promptly do it. No one ever asked Bada Babu if he was making a commission from LIC for selling its products. Everyone sought and trusted his advice on financial matters, on which kind of leave to take, and when. He knew all the arcane rules of the government, and helped everyone with it.

In my first year at work, Bada Babu met me one

March morning as I was hurrying into the hospital. After telling me, to the last paisa, my salary for the year, how much tax I owed the government and what I could do to save it, he asked, 'Sir, what are you doing this Mahashivratri?'

'Nothing, Bada Babu,' I told him.

'Then come to my house for dinner, Sir. We have a big programme every year on Mahashivratri at the Tarakeshwar Nath Mandir near my house. The khichdi they serve for prasad is famous all over Pakur.'

I knew no one in Pakur and, on my off days, I would keep myself from obsessing about Samir by reading, or watching movies on my laptop, and ordering books and DVDs online. Any chance to go out and, especially, to eat something other than boring restaurant food was welcome. I agreed quite readily.

That day, I had the 2–8 p.m. shift at the hospital. We had worked out a plan. Bada Babu had also invited a colleague and Bada Babu would take him to his house on his motorcycle at around 7:30 p.m. I would join them later, after I came back from duty. Since this was my first visit to the area, Bada Babu had given me directions right up to the Tarakeshwar Nath Mandir, where he would meet me.

Unluckily, and quite uncharacteristically for that hospital, I had a busy shift that day. The emergency room, empty until 7.30 p.m., filled up with patients all of a sudden. In just twenty minutes, one after the other, I saw two cases involving seven: one with maar-peet injuries and the other a motorcycle accident, a drunk-driving case. I was fuming. Now I would have to eat once more in a restaurant, I thought. However, I threw all negativity out of my mind and worked hard. The doctor in charge of the night shift came at 7.45 p.m. sharp but though we worked together, I couldn't leave before 8:30 because of the policemen who had come with the patients and brought with them a mountain of paperwork that had to be completed. In between, I kept getting calls from my colleague and Bada Babu.

'Abey, are you are coming or should I eat up your share of khichdi as well?' my colleague asked me.

'Yes boss, I am coming.'

'Aa rahe hain na, Sir?' Bada Babu asked me.

'Haan, haan,' I replied, my mobile phone pressed between my ear and shoulder as I furiously wrote out the patients' medical histories and prescribed medicines. 'I've become a little busy right now. Late se ayenge, lekin ayenge zaroor.'

'Theek hai,' Bada Babu said. 'Hum mandir pe aap ka wait karenge.'

I had intended to stop at home to freshen up but decided against it. I was already late. I could very well freshen up at Bada Babu's house. So I kickstarted my motorcycle and left.

I reached Madhyapara. Without stopping at home, I rode through Rajapara, a locality of grand, crumbling old houses and arrogant Brahmins. The alleys were crowded with people in their finery. There were lights and sounds everywhere. And the famous bhajan, 'Arrey dwaarpalon, Kanhaiya se keh do' was playing somewhere at full volume. I didn't understand why a Krishna-Sudama bhajan should be played on Mahashivratri but I didn't wait to find out.

From Rajapara, I reached Tantipara, a run-down neighbourhood of people from the weaver and other unprivileged communities. From Tantipara I was to take a left turn to reach the Tarakeshwar Nath Mandir where Bada Babu would be waiting for me, or so I hoped. I was excited, and relieved, that I had reached.

The mandir could not be missed. Huge red pennants were fluttering around it and the area was awash with light from a bewildering combination sources: halogen floodlights, tubelights wrapped in red and green cellophane, and flashing disco lights. The place was so crowded that I became nervous. Where was Bada Babu?

Maybe because I was nervous, or I was in a hurry to reach, I didn't pause to look around and rode straight on towards the mandir.

'Arrey! Arrey!'

People started screaming. I braked. Someone put his hand on my rearview mirror.

I was so scared that I nearly fell off my motorcycle. I broke out in a cold sweat.

Looking around, I realized that I had ridden right into the space where the devotees had settled down in two rows to eat prasad. That was another use for PWD roads in Pakur. During the bhog time of a puja or a festival, an entire stretch of a road would be turned into a dining area. Devotees would sit in rows on both sides of a road, while volunteers would walk in the middle, distributing the food. Forget a motorcycle, even a bicycle couldn't pass through. There was just enough space for the young men carrying buckets of khichdi and sabji to tiptoe barefoot through the crowd, serving food. And I had managed to ride my motorcycle right into that sacred and congested space.

All around me a babble of angry voices sprang up. I almost broke out in tears.

'Ke eta?'

'Kothay chole aschhe?'

'Who is this person?'

'What is he doing?'

'Doesn't he see people are sitting here?'

I froze and then heard a loud, familiar voice:

'E! Stop! One minute.'

It was Bada Babu!

He held the rear of my motorcycle and started pulling it backwards.

'Sir,' he told me gently. 'You keep the handle straight.'

I followed his instructions.

'Arrey, raasta ta chhad,' Bada Babu shouted to a few young men around us.

Gone was the rotund, buffoonish head clerk of the Sadar hospital of Pakur, ever helpful with doctors and his seniors. Bada Babu assumed a natural authority and looked like a well-known and respected, even feared, figure in the area. As he shouted, the crowd grew silent and moved aside to make space for us to move.

Bada Babu took me to a roadside a little distance away from the temple. So badly was I shivering that he put a burly arm around me and led me to his house.

There my colleague, as portly as Bada Babu, was standing outside the house, his face white with fear, sure that I had been beaten up. Once we reached, however, the two men started laughing uncontrollably, their vast bellies jiggling. They couldn't stop; if one did, he would merely look up at the other and burst out again. It took them a while to compose themselves but, throughout that evening, they would keep breaking out in chuckles. I was so panicked that I couldn't even be angry at the two for having a good laugh at my expense.

After I had washed my face and hands, heaved sighs of relief and drunk a glass of water, we settled down in Bada Babu's living room. First he introduced me to his wife and got his two children to pay their respects. Then he went out to call in some of the boys who had been baying for my blood just a few minutes ago. To them he said, 'These are daktar saab in our hospital. Recognize them well.'

Once the introductions were complete, the boys nodded respectfully. They said 'Pranaam, Sir,' and left to fetch the khichdi and sabji which was being served outside. Since we were special guests, we did not eat like the others; off leaf pattals, sitting by the side of the road, jostling with each other for elbow room. We ate on Bada Babu's stainless steel plates and he had a lot of extras: fried papad; achaar; dollops of fragrant ghee on the hot, steaming khichdi; and sweets at the end of the meal.

Once we had eaten, Bada Babu showed me around. It was a modest but neatly laid out house and the cleanliness and order bore the signs of a woman's firm hand. It had three bedrooms, a spacious dining and living area, a kitchen, a bathroom, a garden at the rear that adjoined the pond, and also a little outhouse. However, the one thing about Bada Babu's house which struck me as odd was that though it had concrete walls, it had an asbestos roof—the chhat-dhalai had not been done. Not just Bada Babu's, all the concrete houses in the

Rani Dighi Patal area had asbestos roofs instead of regular concrete slabs.

Once he had finished showing me around, Bada Babu took us out into the garden at the back which adjoined the Rani Dighi Patal, one of the many ponds in Pakur where, surprisingly, water can be very scarce in summer.

Expansive and confident in his surroundings, Bada Babu told us about the Patal, and about Pakur.

The pond got its name, said Bada Babu, from Rani Jyotirmoyee Devi, once the queen of Pakur. The queen, of course, had to hand over the pond and all her land to the government in the 1970s, when the Privy Purses were abolished, but her name remained associated with the pond. Like many other members of erstwhile royal families in India, the Rani joined politics and even became an MLA from Pakur over multiple terms.

'Sir, Rani bahut achchi thi. She donated land for a college in Pakur and the Kasturba Gandhi Balika Vidyalaya. The stadium in Pakur is named after her. So is the Rani High School, and the Raj High School for Boys.'

I wanted to point out to Bada Babu that in exchange for all her benevolence, the citizens of Pakur kept electing her their representative, but didn't.

'Sir, when my Mausaji first came here, all this area was jungle,' Bada Babu continued. In the 1970s, when Bada Babu's Mausaji, his uncle, made his way to Rani Dighi Patal, it was government-owned land but, as is often the case, the government had forgotten about it. People from the adjoining neighbourhoods would shit on the banks of the pond and wash their backsides in its water. Gradually, towards the end of the 1970s, people began settle down in the area. The land was there for the taking and they simply demarcated plots and built houses. Since no one knew who the land belonged to, there was no question of buying it from anyone.

In the four decades that had passed since then, I could see that Rani Dighi Patal had become densely populated. I could imagine the few wattle-and-daub houses around the pond and how scenic they must have looked. Now the neighbourhood had mud as well as some concrete houses. The road I had taken to reach the mandir had been tarred and well-maintained. All the houses were lit by electric light bulbs and the reflection of the lights shimmered gently in the water.

Bada Babu's Mausaji was one of the first people to start living in the Rani Dighi Patal area. He had found a nice location for himself—right next to the pond and only a few feet away from the Tarakeshwar Nath Mandir. When Mausaji built his house in the 1970s, it was a simple mud structure, and it remained so till the early 2000s. Mausaji was childless, so he adopted Bada Babu. Mausaji used to work as a clerk in a sarkari office in Pakur. After Mausaji's death in harness, Bada Babu was given the job of a clerk in our office on compassionate grounds.

I wondered to myself how Bada Babu, drawing a government salary, had managed to convert the humble mud house into a brick-and-concrete structure within a few years. My own father, who worked in the copper company at a much higher post, had had to take loans from the company and it had taken him years to build our house in Ghatsila.

I remembered an earlier thought and asked, 'Bada Babu, how do you manage to live under an asbestos roof in summer? Doesn't the heat become unbearable?'

'We don't worry, Sir,' Bada Babu said with a smile, pinching a Navy Cut between his thumb and forefinger, as if he was smoking a bidi, and taking a deep drag. 'We are simple people, not officers like you. We can live in any situation, whether heat or cold.'

We all laughed. And he could have very well been right, he needn't have worried about the blazing heat of the Pakur summer. I looked up and saw the three large trees that spread their canopies over the garden. One towering mango tree sent a large branch over the roof and provided shade. I then looked out over the pond; the ruckus from the Tarakeshwar Nath Mandir was muted and I could almost hear the water lapping the edges of the pond. That March night, as I sat in the garden with these new friends, with a cool breeze blowing over the surface of the pond, I felt a degree of peace. Bada Babu was a lucky man to live beside this pond, I thought.

~

After that Mahashivratri, the floodgates opened. Bada Babu would invite me home almost every Saturday—when he had the day off and I didn't have OPD duties. He had developed a special liking for me. I don't really know why. Maybe he wanted to keep on my good side, given my father and his political connections. Or he wanted his cronies and underlings at the office to know that a daktar babu regularly visited his house. Maybe he just wanted to befriend me. Whatever the reasons, things worked out well for me. For while my duties at the hospital kept me busy enough, my off days were miserable and lonely.

Saturdays at Bada Babu's house were special because that was khichdi day. Bhabhiji, his wife, would cook the khichdi and make sure to keep a large extra portion for me. Bhabiji was a complete contrast to Bada Babu. Slightly built, quiet and self-possessed, she would walk in and out of the kitchen carrying extra helpings of everything, and we would scarcely know that she was there. Inside the house she wore mostly nighties and faded cardigans in winter. Bada Babu's Saturday khichdi was an elaborate affair, not the simple fare we had eaten on Mahashivratri. His appetite and his desire to entertain guests were as huge as his paunch and rump. So I would be served khichdi, cooked to perfection, topped with large dollops of ghee. Aaloo-chokha—boiled potatoes mashed with salt and slightly sautéed in mustard oil with slices of onion and chillies, with sprinklings of turmeric and spices—was a usual side dish. And bhujia, usually slices of brinjal deep fried in mustard oil—a complete health hazard but delicious. Papad and pickles to go with everything, and Navy Cuts after we were done eating.

It was on special occasions like Holi and New Year's Day that parties at Bada Babu's house got very raucous and wild. A few of his favourites from the hospital would be invited home. There would be the portly colleague of mine; the attendant of the X-ray department, a young man but very resourceful, who always had free time on his hands because the X-ray machine never worked; and also another grade-four employee who was Bada Babu's right-hand man, and his eyes and ears in the hospital.

On those special days, we would not eat in the living room. Dhurries and palm-leaf mats would be spread out in the garden behind the house, and our gatherings would happen there. Bhabiji was never involved in these parties and Bada Babu would do all the cooking himself. He would get his right-hand man to help and, together, they would take over the outhouse in the garden, cooking on a clay chulha instead of on LPG. And what dishes Bada Babu made!

On one New Year's Day, Bada Babu had a special

request: we were to start with breakfast at his house and once our shifts ended, we were to go to his house for lunch and stay on until evening.

For breakfast at Bada Babu's that day I took one bite of the crisp bhatura with the heavily spiced chhola and I knew I was in for a long day. Once breakfast was done, we made our slow way to the hospital. After our shifts ended, we went back to Bada Babu's house. On my way there I stopped to buy lemons, Gelusil and four sachets of Eno. There was pulao; parathas for those who did not like rice; a dish made out of sinewy desi chicken with gravy to go with the pulao; another chicken dish made of fleshy broiler chicken in a thick gravy to be eaten with paratha; a paneer dish for the vegetarians; and crisp, fried fish as chakhna which accompanied the endless rounds of Blender's Pride whisky. And once the Blender's Pride got in, the worst in Bada Babu would come out.

That day, he was complaining about a senior nurse who would keep going on leave and send his duty schedules haywire. He told me her whole story, how she was connected to some local leader and how he could do nothing to enforce her attendance. And at the end of his tale, he said, 'Sir, gular ka phool aur madam ka boor bahut kismat wala ko hi milta hai.'

I knew the nurse who was the subject of his story and I was embarrassed by what he said about her—that the good fortune of attaining the rare gular flower, or the cunt of the nurse in question, fell only to the very lucky. And so loudly did he say it that I was afraid his wife might hear him. But even if Bhabiji heard him, or was bothered by his remarks, she showed no sign of it.

That New Year's evening I left my motorcycle at Bada Babu's house, staggered home and crashed into bed. Fortunately, I didn't need the Eno or the Gelusil. And I used the lemons later, in February, when I found that they had ripened and become brown.

A few days before Holi, about two years later, I got yet another call from Bada Babu inviting me to yet another party at his house. And Holi being a gazetted holiday, he asked me to spend half the day with him, from breakfast until lunch.

I was sad that season. Holidays used to have that effect on me. I would remember the wild parties of the medical college on Holi, the bike rides with Samir to the resorts near the Subarnarekha river, the drinking and the sex afterwards. It was bad enough to make me want to shut myself up in my house and not go anywhere.

And, to be honest, I was getting tired of Bada Babu's XXL-size parties. I had become a fixture in his house on every occasion: New Year, Holi, one Diwali when I didn't go home to Ghatsila, children's birthdays. These, apart from the regular Saturday lunches and drinking bouts. We had settled down into a routine. The party would start with whisky—Blender's Pride, or White & Blue which we had recently discovered—and finish with it. The whisky would be accompanied by vast quantities of rich and oily food, conversations that went around in drunken circles, dirty jokes, and innuendoes about doctors, nurses and other staff at the hospital. There would be masses of food to consume and, equally, a lot that would go waste, which I couldn't bear.

That Holi, the decision was taken out of my hands. A ward-boy in the hospital, whose son I had treated for a minor infection, invited me for breakfast. And Mishra Ji, my landlord, extended me a special invitation for lunch.

I went to both places. At the quarters of the ward-boy I was served simple food—malpua, a sabji, a chicken dish, and papad. He asked me if I would like some liquor but I refused. It was too early in the morning to drink. I do not really like playing with colours but that man, my subordinate in the hospital, was so happy that I had come to his house that I let him polish my face a deep pink even though I was wearing a new kurta that day. I came back home, washed my face and prepared for lunch at my landlord's place. This was a terrific affair. My landlords were Brahmins, so no non-vegetarian dish was served, but the vegetarian fare too was more than enough. Malpua, pulao, two kinds of sabji, something fried, a delicious traditional dish, dahi-bada, two types of mithai, papad and chutney. By the time I was done, I was so full that I could just about manage to come home and change. I scrolled WhatsApp to send Samir a 'Happy Holi' message but found that he had blocked me. Too depressed to even think, I went off to sleep.

When I woke up after sunset, I found three missed calls on my phone. All from Bada Babu. Finally, Bada Babu called me at 7:30 p.m.

'Kyun Sir,' he slurred, 'now I have become so small you cannot even come to my place?'

I did not know what to say. I stammered, 'Bada Babu, I am so sorry. My landlord had invited me for lunch so...'

I did not dare mention the breakfast at the home of the ward-boy as that would have made Bada Babu very angry.

However, I heard laughter in the background, which meant he had company. I was relieved. He was drunk and distracted and hung up without saying anything more.

~

On the Monday that followed Holi, I regretted my decision of not having gone to Bada Babu's house. I kept telling myself all day that I should have visited, even if it was only in the evening for a few drinks. For Holi that year was the last time I would have seen Bada Babu's house intact; its spacious rooms, the sprawling trees and the lovely garden at the back which opened out on to the pond—our setting for many good times.

That morning, uncomfortably warm as it usually is after Holi, I was sitting at the tea stall opposite our hospital, stuffing myself with oily luchis and viscous, fiery aaloo-potol-tawrkari, when I heard someone saying that the houses at the Rani Dighi Patal were being demolished. I was jolted by this unexpected news. Before I could think anything, our ambulance-driver called me.

'Hello, Sir. Civil Surgeon Sir has asked us to go to Rani Dighi Patal. I am coming to pick you up.'

I was flummoxed.

'Is the situation there so bad that we have to stay on standby?' I asked as I hurried back to the hospital.

'I don't know, Sir,' the driver said. 'Even I am surprised. I have never been to a demolition site on medical duty. We'll come to know only once we reach there.'

I hurriedly gathered my stethoscope and sphygmomanometer, some medicines and the first-aid box, and called up the young attendant of the X-ray department to assist me. He was a local and a useful man to have around. We were a team of three and there had been no chance to ask a nurse to accompany us as all the nurses were either in the field or on their respective duties. We had not even been given a written instruction or order, everything had been communicated only verbally. If any emergency happened, I would have to handle everything myself. I took a deep breath and sent up a prayer.

Our ambulance, a repurposed Tata Sumo SUV, reached Tantipara. There we found ourselves stuck. Bulldozers, after having razed down a number of houses, were parked on the road. Dust from the demolition hung in the air and a large crowd had gathered; mostly people from the Tantipara and Rajapara areas who had gathered to watch the tamasha.

A horde of policemen and policewomen was milling about everywhere. Some, from the state police, were in regular uniform and carrying wooden batons and cane shields. Others, from the Indian Reserve Battalion, were in battle fatigues and carrying guns. One policeman, holding a megaphone, was announcing: 'Hatiye! Peeche hatiye!' But no one seemed to be listening or moving even an inch. The ambulance-driver stopped, unsure.

'Sir, you keep your gaadi here only,' a young, handsome policeman came up to me and said. 'There is no space to park here. Even our vehicles have been parked far away, in Rajapara.'

How sweet! I thought. Since when did the state police become so good? Then I recalled that he was one of the policemen I had prescribed some medicines to when I had been deputed to the police lines.

We parked right there, beside the road in Tantipara. Next to us was a Radha-Krishna mandir. A recorded kirtan played at full volume—a jarring background track to the demolition of people's dreams and homes.

My first thoughts were of Bada Babu. I hurried off to Rani Dighi Patal. I walked past policemen with tear-gas masks hanging from their shoulders. Past administrative officers monitoring the demolition. Past a bulldozer. Past small piles of bricks, clay tiles, pieces of asbestos roofing. Past the Tarakeshwar Nath Mandir. Onto the road where I had almost been mobbed. And there it was.

Bada Babu's lovely house stood forlorn, shrouded in billowing dust, gaping holes where its doors and windows had once been. His household articles and furniture lay in a heap outside his house.

All sorts of people were walking in and out of the rooms. I couldn't see Bada Babu anywhere. I walked in. The moment I stepped inside, two men wedged iron rods near the hinges of a door and, heaving with all their might, prised it off with a loud ripping sound. There was dust everywhere. I looked around and saw that the places where there used to be beds, chairs, tables, utensils, the TV, were empty. This was a space where we had shared much laughter and togetherness and now it was destroyed.

Bada Babu's wife entered, shouting out instructions to the men working there. That day too, she was wearing an old sleeveless nightie, her face, hair and bare arms covered in grey dust. She looked worried and hassled, not at all the prim and proper hostess that I had always seen her as.

'Bhabhiji, where is Bada Babu?'

'There.' She pointed absentmindedly towards the garden at the rear. Then she asked, suddenly alert, 'Why? Is there something to do?'

'No, no, I was asking just like that…' I did not really know what to say.

She then turned away, her attention on more pressing matters. I walked outside, into the garden. The ground was still coloured red and purple from Holi. Bada Babu was hanging on to a grille, surprisingly surefooted for so large a man, trying to untangle an electric cord. In contrast to Bhabhiji he was the picture of composure. I went up to Bada Babu and helped him with the cord. He did not look at me and ignored my presence. I did not know what to say. I was feeling guilty about having avoided him at Holi. And what, after all, could I have said to a man whose house was being demolished? Bada Babu methodically spooled the cord around his arm, went outside and threw it onto their pile of belongings. He did not look at me or speak to me as he walked past. He went inside again and came out holding a washbasin in his arms. After placing the washbasin with his belongings, he started shouting out instructions to the boys to rip off the windows. It was difficult to see that house coming apart. I couldn't bear to look any more and started walking towards our ambulance. As I turned to leave, my eyes went up to the roof of Bada Babu's house. The asbestos sheets were still intact. Now, after all this time, I understood why Bada Babu and the others living around Rani Dighi Patal had no concrete roofs on their houses.

They knew they were squatters on the land. And no squatter in his right mind would carry out the chhat-dhalai on his house.

The chhat-dhalai, especially for a lower- or middle-class family, is the most difficult and expensive part of building a concrete house. It is an exercise that has to be finished in one go; no breaks are allowed. Labourers work in relays through the night. House-owners have to keep up a steady, continuous supply of food, snacks and tea. And, along with the workers, the house-owners have to stay awake all night, monitoring the entire process and ensuring that everything is available. Casting a concrete roof on a house built on land he doesn't own free and clear is an investment no house-owner will make. It was the same with Bada Babu.

As I turned towards the Tantipara main road, where our ambulance was parked, a bulldozer was preparing to raze a big mud house close to Bada Babu's house. The house had been emptied. It used to have clay tiles on its roof, all of which had been removed and placed in orderly stacks some distance away. Only the skeleton of wooden rafters remained. The tamasha-watchers had gathered around the house in an unmoving mass even as one policeman screamed his lungs out over a megaphone: 'Door hat jaiye! Aap sab door hat jaiye.' Some others tried to push the crowd back, away from the site of the demolition. Passing by the crowd, I thought of the former owners. All their belongings—cots, chairs, mattresses, kanthas, kitchen utensils, buckets, mugs, TVs—their entire life was out there on full display under the open sky, before the eyes of the hundreds of people gathered there.

'Jai Shri Ram!'

Shocked, I stopped in my tracks and turned around.

'Jai Bajrang Bali!'

A bulldozer had razed one of the walls but it wouldn't topple over completely. The driver reversed and approached the wall again.

'Har Har Mahadev!'

The wall gave away, but the rafters remained strong.

'Jai Shri Ram!'

For a second I thought that these slogans were being raised by the tamasha-watchers. What did they think was being demolished? The Babri Masjid?

Then I realized that those were not war cries. They were cries of desperation, of solidarity.

I saw some people clamber on to the half-demolished walls and retrieve the wooden rafters that they had been unable to remove earlier. After taking those rafters off, those men got off the wall and signalled to the bulldozer-driver.

As the bulldozer moved forward to demolish another wall of that mud house, the crowd shouted 'Jai Shri Ram'. These were simple people. Uneducated. That was all they knew in the hour of their need—the names of their gods.

As I settled into the front passenger seat of the ambulance, one thing surprised me: the people whose houses were being demolished, they were not protesting. There was no resistance from them at all.

I thought of all such demolitions I had read about. The last one I remembered was from Nagri in Ranchi, where people were being forced to vacate their land so that the government could acquire land to build an IIT or an IIM or something that would raise the profile of Jharkhand at the cost of the lives of its people. There had been great resistance at that time.

Maybe the people in Nagri owned the land from which they were being evicted, that was why they resisted. There was a meme going around on WhatsApp at the time which showed how an Adivasi policeman was being made to evict an Adivasi woman while the woman was bravely fighting back. The photo carried a tagline: 'The government pits Adivasis against Adivasis!'

Here, while the population was primarily Hindu—mostly Dalits—and some Muslim families, the question remained: Why were people not resisting?

I was sitting in the front seat of the ambulance when the driver came up. 'Sir, you are here? We were looking for you there, near Bada Babu's house.'

'Why? What happened now?' I asked.

'Bada Babu has vacated his house. They will now bring it down. Come, let's watch.'

On my way there, a familiar voice stopped me.

'Daktar Babu, kemon achho tumi?'

It was the tiny, elderly woman I knew only as Maasi.

'Aami bhalo. Tumi kemon achho, Maasi?' I smiled and asked her.

'I am all right, Daktar Babu,' she said.

Maasi would come every morning to sweep and clean the room I lived in when I first came to Pakur. I asked her name one day, and she said very sweetly, 'Everyone calls me Maasi, so you too call me Maasi.' Maasi also cooked meals and washed clothes for those tenants who paid her for those services. Since I ate outside all the time and washed my clothes myself, I did not need Maasi for those things.

I had once gone off to hospital, having washed

my clothes and set them out to dry. It began raining and I was sure that all my hard work had been wasted. But when I returned, I saw that Maasi had very properly arranged my dried clothes on a plastic chair outside my room.

One day, after she had scrubbed my room, Maasi told me that she was suffering from gas. I gave her two Omez capsules from my personal medicine kit. I wrapped the granule-filled capsules in a piece of paper and handed to her. The next day she was full of gratitude: 'Daktar Babu, onek bhalo oshudh diyechho. I have no problem today.'

One other time, she told me that she felt weak. I asked her to come to our OPD. In those days, we used to keep phials of folic acid syrup for pregnant women. I gave her one phial. That made her very happy.

I did not know what those medicines meant to Maasi until I left that small room near the railway station and came to stay in Madhyapara. While walking to and from Pakur's only cinema hall, which is in the Tantipara area, I would often meet

Maasi. One day she took me along to show off her house in Rani Dighi Patal—a simple brick hut with its roof half covered with clay tiles and half covered with a blue plastic sheet.

'Daktar Babu, I live with my son and daughter in this house,' she had chirped happily, before telling me how good I was that I gave her such good medicines.

That day, too, surrounded by the policemen and the demolition crew, she started telling everyone excitedly, even the policemen, 'He's such a nice doctor! He gave me medicines. I used to work for him.'

As she prattled on, I looked in the direction of where her house used to be. It was just a pile of bricks, tiles and blue tarpaulin.

I couldn't hold myself back and asked, 'Maasi, where will you live now?'

At this, Maasi's smile vanished, her face crumpled, and she broke down weeping.

'My son bought this land,' she said. 'He bought it five years ago from a man who lived in Hirapur.

Two kottahs he bought. Each kottah cost us 30,000 rupees. 60,000 rupees we spent in buying the land. Then we built our house. We asked that man several times: When will you get our land registered? He said, soon, soon. Then he vanished. We ran from one person to another. We even went to the Bada Babu who works in the hospital.'

'Oh, Bada Babu? Why him, Maasi? And what did he say?'

'You must be knowing him, Daktar Babu. Bada Babu is our mai-baap. He got us everything when we first came here: voter card, ration card. When my son managed the money to buy land here, it was Bada Babu who told us of this plot...'

I was shocked, and so I prompted, 'When you went to Bada Babu, what did he say?'

He said, 'Chinta korbenna, Maasi. Kichu hobe na. Don't worry, this land is yours, it is legal. So what if it isn't registered?'

I kept staring at Maasi, speechless.

She broke down again, 'Look what's happened to us now, Daktar Babu. Akhon ki hobe?'

'Don't cry, Maasi. Things will be fine,' was all I could say as I walked away. Suddenly, my own troubles seemed very small in comparison.

My mind was churning as I made my way towards Bada Babu's house, picking my way through rubble, household articles lying about discarded, I could see people gathered in small huddles, weeping, talking desperately to anyone who would listen, even the policemen. And, oddly, the policemen were listening closely, with a commiserating 'What can be done now?' kind of a look on their faces. And while, as I was to learn later, there had been some confrontation, the police had been remarkably restrained. They did not conduct a lathicharge and the tear gas had not been used at all. I thought this was ample proof that while there are several ways in which the government can screw the country's citizens, it can do so with utmost care too.

It was well past noon when Bada Babu's house was demolished. It did not give away easily. The bulldozer struck it once, then twice, and then the asbestos roof started falling. When the bulldozer hit the house the fourth time, I saw the mango tree above it shaking. All I could think were of those days I had spent in that house.

What did Bada Babu feel when his house was being demolished? Ignominy? Indignation? Resignation?

I could not say. Bada Babu was nowhere to be seen.

Medical-team duties in the field are always uncertain affairs. We had been rushed to the scene of the demolition but had not been told how long we would have to stay, if we would be given food or made to stay hungry. We were still luckier than the police. They had been at the site since 4 a.m. After demolishing one part of the basti, the demolition team went to the other side of the pond. By then it was well past 2 p.m. The driver and I were hungry, so we bought food from a shop in the Rajapara area and sat on a plinth around a banyan tree near a small Kali Mandir to have lunch.

Two senior citizens were sitting on the plinth, discussing the demolition.

'This is bad, Dubey Ji,' said one. 'We have seen this place grow before our very eyes.'

Dubey Ji remained silent.

'Some compensation or rehabilitation should have been given,' the man continued.

'How is that possible, Shukla Ji? They could have been compensated had they owned the land. They did not own the land. They knew they were in trouble.'

'Yes ...' Dubey Ji agreed. 'Also, they were using up all our resources for free. They got that water pipeline, but when we in Rajapara asked for that same water pipeline to at least be branched towards us, no one listened to us. We are paying 135 rupees to the government for water, and those people just got it for free! What has happened is good!'

I was curious and got talking with the two elderly gentlemen.

Nearly four decades after this basti was established, said Dubey Ji, the state government decided that Rani Dighi Patal was an asset to Pakur and it needed to be beautified and developed into a tourism site. So notices started to arrive from the capital in Ranchi to get the squatters evicted. Successive sub-divisional officers of Pakur—the authority responsible for carrying out such evictions—received orders but they were ignored. 'See, this place is a vote bank, Daktar Babu. So you can see who would have stopped the eviction from happening. And while the eviction was postponed, the population only grew.'

'See, Daktar Babu,' said Shukla Ji. 'Before we got Jharkhand, Pakur used to have a Hindu MLA. Pakur, including this area, used to be mostly Hindu so the votes went to him. And that MLA got a road built in Rani Dighi Patal.'

After Jharkhand was formed, the population dynamics in Pakur changed and more Muslims started living in the area. The then MLA, a Muslim man, promised the residents their houses were safe, that they wouldn't be evicted. To prove this, he had water supply connected by the municipality.

Shukla Ji continued, 'Daktar Babu, all this would have continued. It was all the fault of that one woman that the place was destroyed.'

The government, through the district administration, had been sending notices to the squatters for over a decade. The notices did not come addressed to one person, but to all the squatters. The notices came and were ignored—the squatters were in no hurry to vacate, the administration, prompted by the politicians, was in no hurry either. Then, the squatters filed a case in the state high court against the notices and requesting that the basti be regularized. They lost. In less than a minute, the judge of the high court directed the government to get the area vacated.

Even after the judgement, the administration in Pakur kept dilly-dallying for some time. Instructions came from Ranchi and they were promptly overlooked. For the last one year, though, Ranchi showed a strict stance towards this encroachment. Notices after notices were sent to the squatters. The last notice had been sent at the end of February.

On Sunday morning, the SDO of Pakur had himself visited the Rani Dighi Patal area to talk to the squatters there, to ask them to vacate because the bulldozers would come to raze down their houses. He did not announce any compensation, nor did he talk about a rehabilitation plan, but he at least spoke to the people patiently and politely. But the prospect of her house being razed down angered one woman. She angrily grabbed the collar of the SDO and shouted at him. He still did not react, but left quietly with his team. The next thing the people of that area saw was that right from 4 a.m. on Monday, hundreds of armed policemen had surrounded the Rani Dighi Patal area, announcing on the megaphone for the squatters to leave because their houses were going to be demolished. Everything was just so sudden.

If this suddenness was shocking, that the squatters so peacefully allowed the administration to demolish all that they owned stunned me even more. Didn't they have anyone to guide them? They may have lost the case, but they could have at least demanded compensation. Didn't anyone tell them that? One woman had dared to protest. Why didn't anyone else join her?

I asked the two gentlemen, 'Bataiye, didn't anyone help these people? What about their netas?'

'No Daktar Babu, the netas are all looking out for themselves. That fellow, the one who is Bada Babu at the hospital, what is his name, Dubey Ji ... ?'

Without waiting for a reply, Shukla Ji continued, 'See Daktar Babu, all this is mili bhagat. Every one is in on this together. All the netas and their chamchas have sucked the people of this area dry, taking commissions on everything. Even your Bada Babu at the hospital. He has built a nice house in Rajapara, I have heard ...'

Things suddenly began to make sense. Why the boys had run at his beck and call on Mahashivratri, fetching kichdi and sabji. Some of his parties at which people would drop in, and whom Bada Babu would ply with drink and food. The sundry visitors to his house, wanting this or that.

Shukla Ji and Dubey Ji painted a picture of

our Bada Babu as a regular neta in his area, with a finger in every pie. He was the man to go to if someone needed a water connection, or if someone needed to be hooked up to the electricity supply. He also kept tabs on all the properties in his neighbourhood and facilitated sales and purchases, with a commission for himself. He knew all the political leaders of Pakur, and they depended on him to deliver the votes.

Behind the façade of the jolly man, happy to entertain and be entertained, our Bada Babu was a great puller of strings, smartly turning everything he touched into profit. And, like every good schemer, every good neta, he had made himself safe. What I wanted to know was why he hadn't made his escape before the bulldozers arrived, when there was still time.

And I also understood that the people who could have led protests against the demolition had made themselves secure well before the police and the crews arrived. People like Bada Babu, with government jobs and a ready supply of capital. The only people who were left were the property-less, the truly homeless—Muslims and people from the unprivileged castes, daily-wage earners, domestic helps and cycle-rickshaw pullers. They had nowhere to go to. They had been failed at all levels, by the MLAs who used them as votebanks, by people like Bada Babu who gave them false hope and took their money at every excuse. No one advised them to protest. No one advised them to fight back. No one advised them to lie down before the bulldozers. All they could do was to weep and howl as their entire lives were pulverized before their eyes.

We took our leave and returned to our ambulance which was parked in the Tantipara area. The X-ray room attendant had vanished.

Since it was too hot to sit inside the ambulance, the driver and I went to the cool verandah of the Radha-Krishna mandir beside which our ambulance was parked. The recorded kirtan was still playing.

'God is there,' a man who was standing there

said to no one in particular. 'These people have been punished for their sins. How many times we told them, "Don't shit near the pond. We have our temples here." But they never listened. This had to happen.'

I saw the driver listening attentively. After he had finished his tirade, the man came over to us and said, 'You all have come for a good purpose. We are having kirtan here. We will prepare bhog. Please join us for the bhog in the evening.'

After that man had left, the driver told me, 'Sir, this man just blamed these people for making the pond impure. But where else could they have gone to shit? And which god will be happy with such destruction?'

I kept quiet.

The operation ended at 6 p.m. Then, someone turned up with food packets and bottled water. There had been no food or water the entire day and the police personnel had been working out in the sun since dawn. The water was tepid and each packet contained four sweetmeats and one banana.

Several policemen, angry with the meagre fare, refused to take it. 'This is what we get for destroying people's houses?' one of them complained. 'The administration thinks the police is a joke?' The X-ray room attendant, clever fellow, appeared suddenly, carrying five packets of food and three bottles of water.

A few days later, as I was having my usual breakfast of luchi and aaloo-potol-tawrkari outside our office, I saw a huge crowd of people marching on the main road of Pakur.

'They are those whose houses were demolished,' my luchi chef informed me. 'They are going to the DC's kothi.'

'And what do they expect to find there?'

'God knows,' the luchi chef said. 'Their houses have been broken, their lives have been taken away. They are demanding compensation but nothing will be enough now.'

It had rained in the last few days, soon after the demolition. I remembered reading somewhere that after the atomic bombs had exploded in Hiroshima and Nagasaki, it had rained. I also read somewhere that it had rained after the Bhopal gas leak. After the houses around Rani Dighi Patal were demolished, it rained in Pakur, too.

After breakfast I plunged into my duties in the OPD. Sometime in the afternoon, a Muslim woman came to me with her four-year-old son. The boy had cold, runny nose, and sore throat.

'He got drenched in the rain,' the woman explained.

'Didi,' I asked, 'why didn't you stop your child from going out in the rain?'

'Ki kore, Daktar Babu?' the woman said. 'Our houses were broken that day. We are living under open sky now.'

'You… you…' I was quite at loss for words, 'you're from the Rani Dighi Patal area?'

'Yes,' she said. And added, 'We cannot buy medicines. Please give me medicines from the hospital only. His abbu pulls a cycle-rickshaw and he is also unwell.'

~

After his house was demolished, I didn't meet Bada Babu much. He didn't invite me for parties; in fact, I didn't know if he was having any at all. Whenever he would meet me in the hospital, he would avoid my eyes, and just hurry off with a perfunctory, 'Namaskar Daktar Babu.' I had heard from some people that he was living in a rented house, but I did not know where.

On the last day of December, Bada Babu called.

'Sir, agar free hon to kal naya saal manane aiyega?'

I was surprised by his invitation to celebrate New Year but I was also dying of curiosity. I needed to talk to Bada Babu, to ask him a few questions. And that year, without the only diversion I had in Pakur, I had been very lonely. I missed Bada Babu's cooking and his parties, too.

'Zaroor ayenge, Bada Babu,' I told him, and he gave me directions to his rented house in Hirapur.

When I reached that evening, Bada Babu met me at the door. He was fully dressed and it was quite obvious that he had been drinking. Without asking me in, he said, 'Sir, mere saath aiye. I want to show you something.'

I did not know what he was up to. But I got on his motorcycle and off we went.

We reached Rajapara where Bada Babu drove up to a house which looked like it was in the final stages of being completed. It was a large house, far bigger than the one which had been demolished.

We went inside. The house had two storeys and both the floors were complete. There was a small verandah in the front, stairs that led up to the upper storey, a spacious kitchen and an expansive hall, two bathrooms, a smaller space to be made into a puja room, big bedrooms, and a special room—Bada Babu told me—with a personal balcony of its own, for Bada Babu himself. Also, this house had a separate wing with its own entrance. This wing had two suites with one small foyer, a bedroom, a small kitchen, and a small toilet-cum-bathroom. These suites were to be given out on rent.

Bada Babu came up to me, close enough for me to smell the whisky on his breath. 'Sir, today I am very happy. The house was completed two days ago and I really needed to celebrate. That is why I invited you.'

Bada Babu's new house threw up a lot of questions in my mind, the first about money and where he got so much capital from. But I said nothing.

'Sir, this house will be ready soon,' Bada Babu slurred as we walked out of the compound. 'In six months, the house will be complete. I want you to leave the place where you are staying and come and stay with us. One of the suites is for you.'

'Mm—hmm ...' was my only response.

We reached Bada Babu's rented house, a simple two-bedroom affair on the ground floor with a small living room where a divan and a sofa set were clustered around a centre table. A half-consumed bottle of Blender's Pride was standing upon the table. Bada Babu sat down heavily upon the divan and called out for one more glass and chakhna. Bhabiji, in her usual home attire of nightie and cardigan, came out with a plate of fried chicken, a glass, and Sprite. She looked self-possessed once more, and had a smile on her face.

'Namaskar Daktar Babu.'

'Namsakar Bhabiji.'

Formalities completed, she went back inside.

We were on our second round when I asked Bada Babu, 'Didn't you know that the area was going to be demolished?'

'Arrey, leave that no, Sir. Why talk about that now?'

But when I persisted, he said, 'Yes, I did know.'

'Then why didn't you leave before?'

'It would have looked bad. As if I was running away.'

So, as I suspected, all of this was all about saving face. His refusal to acknowledge me when his house was being demolished. The past year which he had spent lying low. This New Year day and his compulsion to show off his new, legally valid, house. Had Bada Babu moved out of his house before the demolition, he would have lost all his clout in Rani Dighi Patal. So he did what was useful to him: he stayed back, kept telling everyone that things would be fine, and kept making quiet moves to secure his own family and future.

I took another sip and said, 'But Bada Babu, you were their leader, no? You could have told them at least about the coming demolition...'

Bada Babu got charged up all of a sudden. 'Arrey forget that, Sir. Everyone knows that stupid woman caused that demolition. Had she not confronted the SDO...'

He paused, drank a big gulp of whisky, and continued. 'And anyway, I am trying my level best to get them land in other parts of Pakur...'

The whisky, which had been tasting very nice until then, became unpalatable to me. There was Bada Babu munching on a piece of chicken before me and, all around him, I could see Maasi, that Muslim rickshaw-puller's wife with the sick child, and that one woman—whom I had not seen and whose face I could only imagine—grabbing the collar of a powerful man wearing a suit in a last, desperate attempt to save her house. They would soon be at his doorstep again, begging him to get them land, and houses.

I somehow gulped down the last of the whisky in my glass and left.

FATHER

I stand on the terrace outside my room. The garden, which my father built, where he obsessively, tirelessly works, is laid out before me, an oasis of green in a neighbourhood rapidly filling up with concrete houses. Each tree, each flower, is sharply lit by the clear light of the morning, which carries the promise of a hot day. I hear the shuffling of slippers. My father comes up and stands alongside me, looking out at his handiwork. He turns to me and I can feel his searching gaze linger upon my face. His eyes travel downwards and rest on my bandaged wrist. My hands clench involuntarily, and a sharp pain reminds me of my wound. Once or twice, I hear him breathe sharply, as if he was preparing to speak, but he says nothing.

~

My father was born in Kessorepur—our village, now in southern Jharkhand—the eldest of all his siblings and half siblings. His father, Dadu, was the majhi, the headman, of our village and the owner of vast tracts of land, which included forest, grazing areas and paddy fields, some of which, said family legend, needed seven pairs of oxen working together to plough. Our granaries were always full and our ponds teemed with fish. Dadu married twice, and had a number of children from both his wives. As majhi of Kessorepur, he was tasked with adjudicating and settling disputes, and most importantly, he was the guardian of the village jaher, the most sacred centre of our faith, where everyone prays during the Baha and Maak Moray festivals. It was his responsibility to ensure, along with the naikay—the village priest who worships the gods—that prayers were regularly offered at the jaher.

In Kessorepur, the jaher was a plot of land, common to everyone, where farming was not allowed. The cutting of trees was forbidden and they flourished there. In the middle stood a huge banyan and at a distance from it were two gigantic sal trees. Under these trees was the heart of the jaher, the shrine of Marang Buru and Jaher Ayo, our chief deities. During the Baha festival, all the Santhals of the village would get together in a procession, carrying some home-brewed haandi as offering and some sindoor for the shrine, and, with the majhi at its head, first make their way to the house of the naikay. The naikay would then be escorted to the jaher, heralded by drumbeats, music and songs, where he would pray to Marang Buru and Jaher Ayo for the prosperity of the village and for protection from the malevolent deities.

As majhi of Kessorepur, the welfare of the village was Dadu's responsibility, and so was its jaher, but he was fated to walk a different road.

The scion of the principal family of the village, Dadu was the first boy from Kessorepur to attend school in Chakulia, the town closest to the village, which he could not complete. And the way in which he was kept from education had already become part of family lore by the time I was born.

In those days most teachers and students came from the privileged upper classes and castes. For Adivasis to attend school was rare and, to many there, Dadu was merely a village Santhal boy, an untouchable. It mattered little that he was the son of the headman of Kessorepur. Let alone coming into physical contact with him, teachers would speak to him from a distance, and not even look at him when they did so. His classmates too were no better.

Dadu bore the taunts and discrimination patiently until, one day, he reached breaking point. A teacher accidentally dropped a blackboard duster on the floor. When Dadu picked up the duster to give it back, his teacher became furious and shouted, 'Insolent boy! How dare you touch that? Now I can't use it again!' In anger, he flung a piece of chalk at Dadu.

Dadu rushed up to the teacher and shoved

him to the floor. He was roundly thrashed and suspended from classes.

That same evening, he packed up his things and walked out of the school hostel. He spent the night in a roadside shack. Come dawn, he set out on foot for Kessorepur and reached home by evening.

When Dadu's father heard that he had run away from school after hitting his teacher, he slapped Dadu.

But Dadu said, 'I am not going back ever again.' And nothing could change his mind.

With formal education no longer a factor in his life, Dadu was free to do as he pleased. He was the eldest son of the most important landed family of the village and he had no need to worry about food or livelihood. So all he did now was to roam the world that lay outside the boundaries of Kessorepur—the towns of Chakulia and Baharagora, and further afield, Ghatsila, Mosaboni and Gamharia.

When I was growing up, Dadu would take great joy in recounting the stories of this time, the freedom and the power of that phase of his life.

Everywhere he went, Dadu would say, he found that the discrimination he had faced in school was only a small part of what was happening in Bihar at the time. Santhals were looked down upon by the members of the higher castes and classes as uncivilized people and given all kinds of insulting and humiliating names. However, what angered Dadu most was the humiliation of Santhal women. They were teased and molested on the streets and in marketplaces. There were even incidents of Santhal women being abducted by the sons of rich Bhumihar landowners.

Dadu decided to do something about this and got together a few like-minded Santhali boys. Arming themselves with stout sticks and a few weapons, they formed a gang. Whenever they heard that Santhal women were being exploited somewhere, they would fight with the men who had exploited them. As Dadu described those encounters, his eyes bright and his face flushed, they became pitched battles they fought against people more powerful than them, none of which they lost. And, as time passed, there was no one in any village for miles around who could stand up to these young men. As children, we would listen wide-eyed as he narrated his exploits.

'It was evening, and I was cycling home to Kessorepur. Have I told you that I had the only bicycle in the whole village?'

We knew, of course, having heard this many times, but we nodded silently, eager for the story to continue.

'I looked back and saw a group of men following me. I knew they meant trouble. We had beaten up one of them only a few days earlier. So you know what I did?'

We nodded our heads to say no.

'I untied the stick that I always kept on my bicycle and held it above my head.'

'Then, Dadu, what did you do?' a cousin asked.

'What did I do? I just whirled the stick around my head and ran towards them, shouting at the top of my voice.'

'Then what happened, Dadu?'

'What would happen? They just ran away!'

Of course, looking back, it is easy to see this gang, fighting with people and seeking to avenge the honour of Santhal women, simply as a group of boys who were giving expression to their youth, and their hot blood. But, at the same time, it is also not difficult to imagine that Dadu, and his friends, were caught up in the wave which was then sweeping post-Independence Bihar, a wave that was unifying the Adivasi peoples and which, decades later, would result in the formation of Jharkhand.

It was at that crucial time, when Dadu's energy was at its highest tide, and most in need of channeling, that he came into contact with Jaipal Singh, the Marang Gomke—the Great Leader who had represented all the Adivasi peoples of India in the Constituent Assembly—and who was then relentlessly campaigning for a separate homeland for the Adivasis.

Dadu met Jaipal Singh for the first time at a rally near Chakulia. This meeting was the highest point of Dadu's life, and he would remember it with pride until the end of his days.

'"Join us," Marang Gomke said to me.'

'"Me?" I couldn't believe my ears.'

'"Yes. Come with us. We need young, strong men like you."'

Dadu needn't be asked again. He joined Jaipal Singh's party, first as a worker and, as time passed, he climbed its ranks to become a full-time politician.

Dadu was hardly ever at home even as a young man. Once he joined Jaipal Singh, however, and grew as a man of politics, his work took him all over Bihar and his stays in the village became even rarer. However, any Santhal village is lost without its majhi and Kessorepur was no exception to this rule. Without the majhi to lead the people and perform his duties, the upkeep and cleanliness of the jaher fell away and worship became rare. The gods were neglected and Kessorepur became haunted by fear. In their later years, my father and uncles would describe how an eerie stillness would grip the place by twilight. An utter silence which nothing broke, not the cries of children, not the squawking of roosting birds, or the barking of dogs. If one walked outdoors after dark, he would feel as if someone was following him. No one would venture out, even to relieve himself. And where there is fear, rumours breed rapidly. People in the village began to believe that many were turning to Sima-bonga, the malevolent god of the jaher, who bestows great wealth upon whoever propitiates him, but who also destroys his acolyte's health and peace of mind. They all began to believe that it was because of Sima-bonga that Kessorepur had begun to feel unsafe after dark and, soon, any illness and death in the village was believed to have been caused by Sima-bonga. This belief sowed the seeds of doubt and people who had long been neighbours began to view each other with suspicion. Most disturbingly, it was whispered that the naikay had begun to pay obeisance to Sima-bonga instead of Marang Buru and Jaher Ayo.

Then, on one Baha festival, an incident took place which convinced everyone about the naikay. That year, a festive procession got together but, as usual, my grandfather was away from Kessorepur and absent at the head of the gathering. When the procession reached the naikay's house, he refused to come to the jaher.

'Where is the majhi?' he asked. 'He has become too big to come to my house, to take part in the Baha. And without him, I won't do the worship.' Even though everyone tried to mollify him and get him to conduct the worship, the naikay stayed firm in his refusal.

This shocked everyone, and proved that the village priest of Kessorepur was worshipping Sima-bonga. Why else would he refuse to offer prayers to Marang Buru and Jaher Ayo?

When Dadu came back and the villagers told him what had happened, he became very angry. 'Why, was the naikay using my absence as an excuse?' he asked. 'He knew I was away. He could have easily conducted the Baha on his own!' There were many who understood what Dadu was getting at but he didn't press the matter further. Dadu then impetuously declared, 'If the naikay will not conduct the Baha, we will not have it at all in Kessorepur. And if the gods decide to abandon us, so be it.'

After this declaration, a sharp rift grew between our family and that of the naikay. And with both the majhi and the naikay of Kessorepur ceasing worship at the jaher, as well as the Baha celebrations, that beautiful, serene place became a desolation, wild and overrun with weeds and bushes.

~

Even though he himself couldn't complete school, Dadu's exposure to the wider world of politics had convinced him of the need for education. He sent all of his sons to school and my father became the first boy in the family to finish school and join college in Chaibasa, an important administrative centre to the west of Kessorepur, to study chemistry. College was to prove fateful, for that was where my father had his first taste of politics.

When he was in first year, a scandal rocked

the college. A Santhal girl from the village of Kharsawan, who was in a relationship with a Bihari boy from Chaibasa, fell pregnant by him. But when she asked the boy to marry her, he refused. The girl's guardians tried to intervene, and even spoke to the boy's family, but why would they have anything to do with a Santhal girl? Why would they bring an untouchable girl home as their daughter-in-law? The matter eventually became public and incensed the Santhal students in the college. A group of these students, which also included my father, cornered the Bihari boy one day and tried to convince him to marry the girl. But the boy, sitting on the high horse of his caste, was unyielding, and matters soon got heated. Fisticuffs ensued and the Bihari boy ended up being beaten up quite badly. It was a minor miracle that my father and his friends escaped suspension.

Years later, reminiscing about that time, the golden years of his youth when anything at all had seemed possible, my father would remember that that was the only occasion when all the Santhals of the college had come together. The winds of Adivasi unity were blowing across Bihar, but the Santhal students were anything but united.

For my father, the incident with the girl was only one example of the many ways in which the Santhals were being exploited. After all, Dadu was in politics at that time, a member of a political party that was struggling for a separate homeland for the Adivasis. Some of his political sensibilities would surely have seeped into my father as well. The idea of organizing the Santhal students was an obvious one. So he spoke to the senior Santhal students, suggesting that they should all join forces with the other Santhal and Adivasi students to form a united front. 'Look,' he said to them, 'there is so much unity among the Ho boys. We should join them, and others. Can't you see what all is happening to our girls? We must unite.' Of all the groups among the larger Adivasi community, it was the boys from the Ho community who were the most powerful. They had the force of numbers and they dominated college politics. It was they who had led the group that had tried to get the Bihari boy to marry the Santhal girl.

His seniors responded, 'Arrey, you are only in first year and already you want to do politics? Just pay attention to your studies.'

It was useless expecting anything from his Santhal seniors, so my father began to spend most of his time with the Ho boys, and those Santhal students who believed too that they should be united. He also made friends among the Diku—the non-Adivasi—students as well. This has always been a special quality of my father's: his ability to adapt himself to circumstances, to make friends and alliances, to try and dominate and lead in any situation.

Now part of large group of friends, both among the Ho students and other Santhals, as well as among the Dikus, my father became a popular student in college. Gradually, he became a representative of the students—a sort of a leader, especially among the Santhals—to the college management and teachers. Together, he and his friends also got into mischief. One incident, in particular, always stayed with him and he never tired of telling it, the narration accompanied by much laughter and thigh-slapping.

One of their friends belonged to a modest family from the Dhobi community. The students had once staged a play, a romance between a rich boy and a poor girl, at an annual function in their college. Their Dhobi friend was to play the hero's character, who was the son and heir of a big businessman. In one scene, the hero was supposed to arrogantly ask another character: 'Do you know who I am?' On the day of the final performance, my father and some of his friends climbed up the stage and sat hidden on the rafters. When their friend began delivering his sneering dialogue, 'Tu jaanta hai main kaun hoon?' they all interrupted him with a whistle and shouted loudly: 'Saala, you are the son of a Dhobi!' The play was ruined, of course, but that was the part which the audience enjoyed the most.

A popular student by the time he reached third year, my father decided to do the unthinkable:

he stood for the post of college president. Everyone thought he was mad, for no Adivasi had ever been elected president of that college. But discouragement spurred him on, and he just had to make his point. He canvassed support, networked, and on the strength of his popularity, beat the odds to be elected the first-ever president of that college.

After he graduated, my father found a job as a chemist at the copper company in Ghatsila. Soon after he joined, he fulfilled a long-held ambition and bought himself a 250 cc Yezdi motorcycle, his prize and joy. Now holding a secure job with prospects of growth, Dadu was keen that my father got married. He found my father a bride from Jamshedpur. At that time, my mother was still in high school, studying science. After they got married, my father made sure she appeared for the medical entrance exams and enrolled in medical college—years later, he was to do the same for me. While my mother was still completing her house-surgeonship in the college, he got her to apply to the hospital in the copper factory, where she became a doctor, a position she held for the duration of her working life. And it was in the large, Raj-era bungalow which she had been allotted as residential quarters by the copper factory that we all lived in until she retired from work. I, the only child of my parents, was born when my mother was still studying at the medical college, delivered by one of her professors even as my father and her classmates waited anxiously outside the labour room.

~

Many years had passed since my father had left Kessorepur to find his place in the world. In all the time that he was away, the affairs of the village were very much on his mind. He always worried about Kessorepur: a village whose two most important guardians, the majhi and the naikay, refused to have anything to do with each other. A brief hope was kindled when Dadu, ageing, and disillusioned by the politics which had all but destroyed the movement for a separate homeland for the Adivasis, had begun to spend more and more time at home. But that hope soon died, for he took no interest in his duties, or in the affairs of the village. It was as if all his energies had been consumed by politics and he had no more left.

Today, my earliest memories are not of Ghatsila but of Kessorepur. The large ancestral house, the trees around it, the jaher which was forbidden to us, my many cousins, uncles and aunts. I remember Dadu, still an imposing figure, seated on a cot, benevolent but distant. None of us children would even dare strike up a conversation with him. He himself spoke but rarely to us, and when he did, it was only to recount to us the stories of his youth which would keep us spellbound. I also remember the many rules which were imposed upon us children. Some, of course, were to prevent me, unused to the rough village ways, from falling into harm's way, but others only made themselves clear to me later, after I had grown up and understood what had befallen our village.

One of my aunts might say: 'You are not to go

near the jaher.' Or, 'If I see you all anywhere near that house, I will break your legs.' And, as twilight fell, someone or the other would stand at the doorway of our house and shout at us to hurry back inside. If we delayed, or stayed back to complete a game, we were sure to get a cuff on the head.

'This cannot continue,' my father said to Dadu one day. 'Things have to change. Kessorepur cannot be allowed to go to ruin like this. What will we tell our children when they grow up? We have to do something.'

'Do what you must,' Dadu replied. 'But whatever happens, don't beg that naikay to help us out.'

'We don't need that naikay,' my father told Dadu. 'I have found one in our own family.'

After I grew up, and understood these things better, I always wanted to ask Dadu what he felt about his son taking on the duties of the village headman and guardian even when he was alive—didn't he feel like he had been usurped? Did he not care about that at all?—but I never dared.

At the same time I can see clearly that my father

took his duties as the eldest son of the headman's family seriously. He is just that sort of man—with an innate sense of responsibility, and a desire to assert himself in any situation. He has always believed, whether at work or in our house, that if something has to be done, he is the one to do it. And who knows, maybe he could see that Dadu was a spent force; that, having been in the whirl of politics in Bihar, Dadu just wasn't interested in being the headman of tiny Kessorepur anymore.

When he was still a student, there was little my father could do. But now, a man with a job in the copper factory in the city, and the head of a young family, he commanded respect in Kessorepur. We would visit the village on the Durga Puja and Diwali breaks at my school. Many men, especially the young, would come up and offer my father their respects. My father would gravely receive their johar, and advise them to study hard and attend college if they were to get jobs. But he would also talk to them about his childhood—how lush and beautiful the jaher had once been, how men and animals stayed healthy and productive until the end of their days. A time when one could walk about everywhere fearlessly. He told them that the only way Kessorepur would become what it once was if the jaher was restored. Some among the younger generation were inspired by his words and they gradually set to work.

My father had a vision for the jaher. He wanted it to return to its original form, a dense, orderly forest, not overrun with wild shrubs, and with a few grassy spots where people could cook the bonga-soray—the sacrificial meal of mutton, chicken and rice—on festival days. The bushes and undergrowth in the jaher were cleared so that people could walk about. A hedge of bushes and bamboo strips was put up to keep out stray cattle and other animals. The sal trees under which the worship took place were already there. My father decided that there should be more of these magnificent giants in the jaher and so he planted some saplings himself. He saw that shady trees were needed so he planted neem and fig. For fruit there were mango and star fruit trees. No jaher is complete without flowering shrubs and so some of the wild lantana bushes were uprooted and replaced by hibiscus and other plants. This took years, and much investment of effort and his own money, but my father persisted. In a way, this was the first garden that he created.

With the jaher gradually recovering its past glory, my father convinced his uncle, Dadu's younger brother, to take on the role of the naikay. Regular worship began again and, on the Baha festival, a procession would gather to take Dadu and his younger brother to the jaher.

Did the restoration of the jaher have any effect on the well-being of Kessorepur? Who can tell, now that it is a ruin once more, a disaster too painful to contemplate? But one thing was certain: the jaher responded to the care bestowed upon it and, until well into my adulthood, it was lush and serene, a place of peace and of power.

~

My father took on the duties of the headman of Kessorepur at the turn of the last decade of the twentieth century. Three important events took place at that time which were to utterly transform our lives.

First, my father was promoted—from a chemist, he was made the manager of a plant. With the promotion, he became eligible for a company loan and, with that money, he fulfilled another great ambition of his: he bought a plot of land in Ghatsila on which he would build our house, and the garden that would become his refuge and escape.

The third, most important, event was my father's decision to join politics. That decision transformed our lives in more ways than one.

As the first Adivasi president of his college, he had already had a taste of power and must have nurtured political ambitions. He certainly had the pedigree for it, for though retired from active politics, Dadu was still very well known and respected, not only among the Adivasi people, but among others too. Most importantly, Dadu and my father both believed in the vision they had been shown by the great Jaipal Singh: that a separate state for Adivasis was the only way in which we could secure our rights in new India.

At that time, an unexpected political formation, the Hindu India Party, declared that if voted to power, it would support the creation of a separate state of Jharkhand for the Adivasis. This set all of Bihar buzzing. The HIP had no Adivasis in its rank and file. Why was it extending its support for a separate state of Jharkhand? Was it merely setting the issue on the boil again, hoping to reap benefit from it? Was it seeking newer votebanks?

But, for my father—and for many other Adivasis of his generation—these were immaterial questions. If a party with a national base had decided to throw its weight behind a separate state for Adivasis, it should be given a chance, they believed. After all, every other national party had, by then, used the struggle for a separate state of Jharkhand for its own political gain and cast it aside. The local parties, too, had done the same. All of them had failed the Adivasi peoples. My father decided to join the HIP. And, as with everything he did in life, once he decided, he threw all his energies into joining the party.

He needed to, for he faced two challenges. He had no experience of party politics and, joining the HIP was no easy matter. The ranks of the party in the Ghatsila area comprised primarily upper-caste Hindus. It had no Muslim or Christian—and certainly no Adivasi—members, and there was resistance from the Hindus about a Santhal joining their ranks.

In the early days, when a party member had asked one of the local Diku leaders to support my father's candidature, he reacted, 'Ab kya yeh nar-vaanar bhi aayega Sabha mein?'

Many years later, I heard my father laughingly recount this story to a friend, one of the only times I ever heard him speak of the discrimination he faced. 'You know, they called me a man-ape when I wanted join the party. I still did it!' But the hurt still remained in his eyes. It was only the first of the names he would be called, for discrimination cuts in many ways. Later, after he had joined the party and become well-known in his constituency, there were several Santhals who took to calling him 'Diku seta', the dog of the Dikus, for having joined a party of the non-Adivasis.

My father had two close friends in the factory—one was a Brahmin and the other a Baniya. Both of them were members, not only of the HIP, but also of other organizations which shared the same ideology as the HIP. Once he told them about his intentions, my father's friends started taking him along to party meetings and events. There, he met other local leaders of the party. These leaders were the prominent Brahmin men of Ghatsila, and the Marwari businessmen and Bhumihar, landowning, contractors who, between them, owned and controlled everything in town: the textile stores, the stone quarries, the ration distribution shops, the government contracts to build irrigation canals and roads. These leaders must have been impressed by my father—a man whom many Adivasis knew was the son of a former politician, an officer with the copper company, and, most importantly, the perfect candidate to field from the Ghatsila seat, which is reserved for the Scheduled Tribes. They inducted him into the HIP.

With my father's induction, and the promise that he would be the party's nominee from Ghatsila in the Vidhan Sabha elections, politics arrived like a whirlwind in our household. My father took extended, unpaid, leave from his work in the factory and started travelling—to the party headquarters in Ranchi, to Jamshedpur, Chaibasa and further afield, meeting leaders and party-workers and getting their advice and support. As time passed, the number of people visiting our house increased—members of the HIP, local leaders and businessmen, party-workers. Some of them offered advice, others came to strategize. And there were those, too, who simply wanted to show their face, in hope that they would be remembered later, once he became the Member of the Legislative Assembly from Ghatsila, the MLA Saab. I watched all of this in a daze. We were a small, self-contained family: my mother, father and an aunt who lived with us. We were used to a quiet, regular life, dictated by the routines of my school and the sirens of the factory. To me, still a schoolboy, these visits, and all the coming and going, were very exciting.

Any election campaign costs a lot of money. There were posters and flyers to be printed. Once printed, they had to be pasted all over town. There was also the material which had come from the party headquarters and had to be distributed. With the material came party-workers from Jamshedpur, Ranchi and Dhanbad. They had to be found lodgings, which my father paid for. The workers would be out all day, campaigning, but once they returned after sundown, all of them would eat their meals in our house, cooked, of course, by my mother and aunt. The HIP was well known as a party of the prosperous but it left the entire burden of financing his campaign to my father.

At this time, when my father was spending less and less time at home and plundering his life's savings to fuel his political ambitions, it was my mother who kept our home fires burning. She bought large quantities of groceries, helped out with the cooking, and supervised my schoolwork. And, on her off days, she would get together with women party-workers and go door to door, canvassing for the party and for my father.

At that time, the HIP was relatively unknown in my father's constituency, which comprised the towns of Ghatsila and Mosaboni. These areas were staunch, at times violent, partisans of local parties. The citizens here spoke the Santhali, Mahali, Ho and Mundari languages; Bangla in local dialects; even Odia. The workers whom the party had sent spoke mainly Hindi and were ineffectual. So my father took matters into his hands and rode his Yezdi everywhere, the party flag strapped to his rearview mirror, meeting people.

Once, as my father and his friend were travelling through a Santhal village, a few men blocked their way. This was a village which had historically supported a local party. Putting a hand on the party flag which fluttered on the front of the bike, one man asked, 'Whose flag is this? Why are you here? Don't you know which party we vote for?'

My father was intimidated but he stood his ground. He got off the bike and parked it on the side. Then, speaking in Santhali, he began, 'See, dada ...' He introduced himself, his friend, and explained that he was the HIP candidate. The men were impressed that the party's candidate was himself travelling on a bike, talking about his party. They invited my father and his friend to the shade of a large bakul tree in the village and offered them some water to drink. More people gathered around and they spent a happy half-hour, chatting. My father knew that these people would never vote for him. However, he had the satisfaction of being the only representative from his party to have gone into that village. Any other party-worker from the HIP would have never gone anywhere close. They would have called the villagers nar-vaanars and given them all a wide berth. After having gained entry into that strict Santhal village, my father was certain that it wouldn't be too long before he would get the HIP into every Santhal village in the area.

While my father was working hard to establish the party in his constituency, it didn't help him with much resources. Instead, it gave him star campaigners.

The right-hand man of party supremo came by train and had a picture taken with my father at the railway station which was printed on posters and pasted all over Ghatsila.

An actor famous for his bombastic acting style arrived by helicopter, a glorious spectacle in our small town. I still remember standing with my mother and aunt, along with hundreds of others, waiting for a glimpse and an autograph. My father, of course, was running about making last-minute arrangements and had no time to take us to meet the actor. There was no chance for an autograph. The helicopter landed and the actor was rushed on to the stage. After he made a thundering speech extolling the virtues of the HIP and what it stood for, mentioned my father's name and hectored everyone to vote for him, he was hustled back into the helicopter and flown away.

My father came fourth in the Vidhan Sabha elections that year. But he was happy. An outright win had always been unlikely. Not only was he a rank outsider to politics, his constituency was the stronghold of rival parties. Yet his hard work had paid off. He had increased his party's vote-share and, more importantly, he had become a well-known face in his constituency.

The party's headquarters in Ranchi took notice. Why wouldn't they? For here was a very useful man: an Adivasi, the perfect candidate to field in reserved seats; well-known as someone from a political family; and, most importantly, hardworking and willing to put his own money into campaigns. He was made zila adhyaksh, the district secretary, of the party's rural zone comprising the Ghatsila, Mosaboni, Chakulia and Baharagora areas. For my father, being made the zila adhyaksh was a high accolade as well as a stepping stone to bigger positions and more success. A wave of jubilation swept over the household, and over Kessorepur as well. The family would soon boast of an MLA.

His faith in the HIP stronger than ever, my father set his sights even higher. He was convinced that if the party came into power in the Centre, that it would carve out a separate state of Jharkhand from Bihar. Indeed, this promise was the one constant in every campaign, every meeting, every rally that my father organized. My father hoped that if he managed to become an MLA, who knew, he might even become a Member of Parliament from a brand new state.

As the millennium reached its end, my father started putting all of his energies into politics. He travelled extensively in his constituency, making himself available to everyone. He built formidable contacts everywhere in local politics and the bureaucracy. If there was anyone in his constituency who needed anything—voter and ration cards, intervention with the police, attention from doctors in government hospitals, benefits from government rural schemes—they would come to him. There was an endless stream of people coming and going at home. The tireless energy he poured into his constituency was matched by his zeal for party work. He did everything that was asked of him and more.

Then, something happened which was to change everything.

In one of the elections to the Lok Sabha, the HIP decided to field a Santhal woman from the Jamshedpur seat—the wife of a member of a rival party who had switched loyalties to the HIP. My father who, as zila adhyaksh of the party was responsible for ensuring that the party candidate was well known to everyone in his constituency, was taken aback. Everyone knew the candidate's husband had been a member of the rival party and it would be hard to erase that knowledge from people's consciousnesses. Yet he and other party-workers gave it their all: they worked tirelessly, travelling from village after village, holding meetings and rallies, going door to door, to inform people that their candidate—and her husband—

were no longer members of the rival party but were now with the HIP. It was a difficult job, but they did it. The lady won the election. It seemed an auspicious beginning, for my father would need the couple's endorsement of his candidature for the upcoming Vidhan Sabha elections. And after the victory, our families became close and, in our house, the couple became valued visitors, my father's new Dada and Boudi.

However, this time, the government lasted only a few months and fresh elections were announced. The cycle began again. The HIP fielded the same candidates as earlier, my father campaigned for them as vigorously as earlier, and all of the party's candidates won. In the Centre, too, the HIP came back into power as part of a coalition government.

Everything was going my father's way. The candidates he had campaigned for had won and the top brass of the party supported him. His Dada and Boudi—now the MP from Jamshedpur—were fully behind him. What could possibly go wrong? What could possibly keep him from winning the election and becoming an MLA? And, who knew, maybe a ministerial berth wasn't too far away either.

My father's candidature seemed a foregone conclusion much before the dates of the Vidhan Sabha elections were announced. He was projected as the candidate of the party. Everyone in Ghatsila, from senior leaders and party members to businessmen and shopkeepers, knew him and said that he was the best candidate possible. At the factory, all of his colleagues, and workers, supported my father. In the hospital, my mother's patients, and everybody else, told her that they would vote for her husband. Even a few teachers in my school addressed me as the son of the new HIP neta. I was thrilled.

Party-workers were mobilized, posters printed and pasted on walls, rallies and sabhas organized. My parents, whenever they were at home, discussed nothing else but the elections. For a while, I receded into the background of their lives.

It seemed as if nothing could stop my father from becoming the MLA from Ghatsila. There was only one worrying cloud—the party had not officially announced his name as their candidate.

The dates of the elections were announced, as was the date for the candidates to file their nominations. All the parties except the HIP announced the names of their candidates. My father was in constant touch with the top brass of the party in Delhi and Ranchi.

'Yes, yes,' he was told by everyone. 'Aap ko hi ticket milega.' My father would be reassured. Hadn't he worked hard for the party and ensured it was now well known in the rural constituencies? And didn't he have the support of his Dada and Boudi? Nothing could go wrong.

Finally, the date for the filing of nominations arrived. The HIP was yet to announce its candidate and my mother was nervous, but my father's confidence was sky-high.

'Let us file the nomination first,' he declared. 'They will announce my name sooner or later.'

We all walked to the Sub-divisional Officer's office in a large procession which included nearly everyone from the Ghatsila unit of the HIP, as well as workers, officers, doctors, nurses and other employees of the copper factory. After his nomination was filed, the campaigning intensified. My mother had to take leave from work to help out full time. Everyone was excited. I was excited, and so was my aunt. 'If your father wins, where will we live? In Ghatsila or in Patna?' she asked me gleefully. I knew as much as she did—nothing. And though I liked Ghatsila, Patna was the capital, and the big city. It might be nice too.

The first shock came just a few days after my father filed his nomination. The newspapers reported that a Santhal man, a rank newcomer, had filed his nomination as the party's candidate from Ghatsila. My father knew nothing about him, or his nomination. He had been kept completely in the dark. He then found out something even more devastating. That man had been inducted into the party by his very own Boudi.

Then came the next jolt. The HIP announced that the newcomer would contest the elections from the Ghatsila seat on the party's ticket.

My father protested. He called the headquarters in Ranchi, he even spoke to his contacts in the Centre. His campaign had reached an advanced stage, he said to everyone, and he had invested much effort and money in it. And, more importantly, changing the candidate at this late stage would confuse the public and hurt the party's chances in Ghatsila. No one listened. And, as the elections approached, everyone in the party stopped taking his calls. Having exhausted every possibility of intervention, and having been stonewalled everywhere, he quietly withdrew his nomination.

Once the news of his withdrawal spread, many friends and supporters visited and commiserated. Laughing, he said the same thing to everyone, 'It was nothing. Just a fever that did not last long. All it did was make me sweat and then it went away. The party decided and they know best.' But we, at home, knew he was shattered by the betrayal.

Then, one Sunday afternoon, a campaigner for the HIP arrived in town. A grand rally had been organized for him just a stone's throw from our house. The doorbell rang and I went outside.

A loyalist of Dada, for whose wife my father had campaigned for with so much zeal, stood outside the gate, sweating in the heat, looking nervous. 'Beta, aapke Papa se milne aayen hain. Tell him Uncle has come to invite him to the rally.'

I ran back inside. My father was standing next to the door, peering out from behind the curtain, muttering something. I looked up at his face and started to speak, but stopped myself.

I went outside and lied: 'Uncle, Papa ghar par nahi hain. When he comes back, I'll tell him you had come.' I then ran back before he could say anything.

As expected, confusion reigned on the day of the voting. A few people came by after the polls ended. One complained, 'I didn't know what to do. I looked for your name and thought there must be some printing mistake. So I didn't cast my vote.'

In the general melee, votes were divided and the party lost in Ghatsila.

But, that year, the HIP was part of a coalition government in the Centre, and it kept its campaign promise. A separate state of Jharkhand was declared. Only, it brought no joy to anyone in our house.

Of course, things became clear to me later, after I had left home for college and distance allowed me time to think. My father must have presented a threat with his increasing popularity, his zeal, and his ambition. He wasn't going to rest at becoming the MLA from Ghatsila, he would surely try to become an MP, whether from Jamshedpur or any other Lok Sabha seat in Bihar. Insecure, his Dada and Boudi had worked behind the scenes to scuttle his chances.

~

That year, my final exams were coming up. I would be sitting near the window in my room, solving physics problems, mugging up reactions in chemistry, reading stories, or daydreaming.

'Haraamzada ...' 'Maadarchod ...' I would hear

these words, whispered in my father's voice, words which I had never heard him utter.

He would be standing on the verandah outside the window, in his vest and pyjamas, his hands on the grille, alternately staring out at nothing, then muttering. The first time I saw him like this, I felt shock and grief, and also a little fear. He was the strength of our little family, the force which kept us going. He directed our lives, and decided everything for us. Even at the risk of a scolding, I would always turn to him whenever I got stuck with a difficult problem, whether in math or physics or chemistry. To see him unravelling sent a spike of fear shooting through me.

And though the pressure of the exams was upon me, weightier still were the thoughts and feelings crossing my mind, which I did not know how to deal with. Since I had entered teenage, I had found myself becoming attracted to boys in school, to seniors and juniors, but couldn't find the courage or the words to express my attraction to them. I was spending a great deal of time collecting

Filmfare and *Cine Blitz* magazines, from which I cut out photographs of Salman Khan, Akshay Kumar and Abbas and secreted them away in an album. But, most of all, was the great sense of disquiet I felt whenever I thought of my father, and what he would think if he knew what was going through his son's mind. I loved him, and perhaps he loved me too, though he was never a man to say that to me. But I knew what he expected of me, how disappointed he would be if he ever came to know that his son wouldn't become the man that he thought he should be. Disappointed, yes, but what if he rejected me? This was a thought that never ceased to chill me to the bone.

Usually, my father would keep himself busy, at work in the copper factory or tending to his organizational work. He was still the zila adhyaksh of the HIP. And, outwardly, he performed all his duties with the same zeal and the same smile on his face. But the great drive that once defined him was gone. He would take frequent days off from work and spend them at home, sitting at the dining table doing nothing, or mindlessly watching television, tuned to a film or news channel. These stupor-like routines would be broken by him shuffling out to the verandah in his slippers and his awful, whispered swearing. He would then turn around and shuffle back slowly into the house, as if nothing had happened. Thumbing my books, pretending to study, but secretly watching him, I would feel a great wave of helplessness and panic wash over me. But there was nothing I could do. Ours was not a relationship of equals, of friendship. He would never share the grief and the anger he felt, especially with me.

There was one other great change that came over my father. He used to be a fan of sophisticated cinema. The film club of the copper factory would screen many great works, the films of Jahnu Barua and Goutam Ghosh, French and Polish classics; he would watch them all. After his defeat, he would sit hour after hour watching Hindi and Bengali action films, those starring Mithun Chakraborty or Akshay Kumar and Suniel Shetty. And in the climax, when the hero beat up the villain, he would become emotional and pump his fist in the air, his eyes moist, muttering, 'Maar saale ko, maar!'

~

If the party needed anything in Ghatsila—renting grounds and setting up stages for rallies by visiting netas and party functionaries, making sure that crowds turned up for their speeches, fixing the leaders' stay and entertainment in dak bungalows and the Circuit House afterwards—it would turn to my father. He, of course, would do everything. To everyone, he portrayed the image of a man whose only loyalty was to the sangathan, the organizational framework of the party, who didn't care about who was contesting elections and who was winning or losing. And if anyone asked him about standing for elections, his future political plans, he would repeat his standard line, 'It was nothing. Just a fever that did not last long. It won't come back.'

Whenever he would be asked to organize an

event, he would set up everything and, as soon as the event began, he would hand it over to the younger cadres and slip away. On those days, he wouldn't come home, to the factory campus. He would go to our new house, lock up the main gate, and tend to his garden. If anyone came around asking for him, we would simply say that we didn't know where he was.

The house had long been completed by then but remained empty. I used to often wonder why my father didn't put it out on rent but, after his defeat, I understood. The house, and his garden, were his refuge, his shelter. And to me, struggling with the questions in my head, my anxiety, and the looming threat of exams, my father's garden began to feel more and more like a reprieve. Better that he works there, I would think, than sit at home watching television and swearing.

On weekends we would go over to the new house and see the results of his solitary, ceaseless labour. As with everything else in life, my father had meticulously planned his garden too. But unlike his stillborn political career, it had become lush and orderly. Over time, he had bought saplings of sagwan, mango, bananas and guavas and planted them. All these trees were flourishing. Many shrubs and bushes flowered in season; numerous cacti and other succulents in pots lined the garden path.

There was a small shed in one corner in which he kept all the gardening implements in careful order, each one clean and well cared for. He would walk among the tall dahlia which lined the boundary wall, checking for pests, occasionally bending down to pull out a weed. There were roses in many different colours—deep pink, brick red, yellow—planted in pots on the edge of the driveway. They received special attention—regular pruning, fertilizing and mulching. The trees would need trimming, and if they were in fruit, careful scrutiny to see that bats and squirrels weren't getting at them. There were fortnightly trips to his favourite nursery from where sacks of manure, sprays and repellents of all kinds would be brought home. I would help him carry them in at times but he did everything else himself. There was the constant digging and hoeing and weeding. And, other than in the monsoon season, there were endless rounds of watering which comprised an unvarying set of activities. The tubewell pump had to be switched on, lengths of PVC pipe had to be brought out of the shed, uncoiled and connected together in a network precisely designed to reach the last potted plant, the furthest tree, every little patch of grass. Once the watering was done, everything would have to be put away again.

On these visits, I would carefully scrutinize my mother's eyes as they followed my father around the house and the garden. I could see the concern, the bewilderment and helplessness in them too, but we never spoke of it. With my exams around the corner, maybe she wanted to spare me the stress. And, after the exams ended, there was no time.

~

My father had always wanted me to follow in my mother's footsteps and become a doctor. And, in the matter of my higher education and career, he put in the same single-minded energy with which he had once entered politics and which he now lavished on his garden. Perhaps he wanted to ensure that, just like his garden, he would control this aspect of my life to the last detail.

While I focused on the final exams, he collected information about pre-medical entrance tests and had me apply to each one all over India. Prudently, he had also applied on my behalf to courses in science subjects. The only exam which I could choose was the law course at Bangalore University, which he let me make only because I insisted and he wanted me to sit for the final exams undistracted. And once the exams ended, he took leave once again from work and we went everywhere, to Kolkata, Lucknow, Aligarh, Delhi, Bhubaneswar, Ranchi, so I could appear for those exams.

I did not make it to any medical college. However, a call letter from BU arrived and all hell broke loose.

'What? You will spend five years there?'

I was surprised. 'Why? It is a good university.'

'You are not going to study law. Wait for some time. You will surely make it in some other entrance exam.'

'Why should I not?'

He glared. For a moment I felt as if he was going to hit me, as if all the bottled-up anger would come frothing out. But he simply kept glaring at me and, declaring loudly, 'I am not to hear anything about you going to study law,' stomped out of the room.

I felt his keen disappointment in me.

But I was saved. A few days later, another call letter arrived. I had been selected to study Chemistry in Lucknow University.

This satisfied my father for the time being. If not my mother's, I would at least follow in his shoes.

I studied in Lucknow for a year and then, quite abruptly, my father called. 'Medical mein tumhara ho gaya hai,' he said, 'Your medical admission is through. Pack your bags and come home.' I had gotten admission into a college in Jamshedpur.

~

I had many theories about why my father was obsessed with his garden. Chief among them was the thought, the hope, that it was his way of keeping in touch with the soil, and preparing for a return to the village. I imagined that he was getting ready for retirement. Tired of life in Ghatsila, I thought, the setting of his failure, he would go back to our village. Perhaps I was hoping for it too, if only for the sake of his sanity. After all, our family still owned a lot of farmland in Kessorepur and my father would have so much more to do there. Yet all of my speculation was just that, speculation. Dadu died in Kessorepur, soon after I joined college in Jamshedpur, and his going away put an end to all thoughts of retirement to Kessorepur.

With the seniormost member of the family gone, my grandfather's younger brother became the majhi of the village. However, news arrived from Kessorepur that while my father's uncle was ready and eager to take on the mantle of the majhi, he refused to remain the naikay. Why would he want to give up his role of the village priest, everyone asked? Everyone remembered how the earlier naikay was reputed to have taken up worship of Sima-bonga, and how he had refused to worship at the jaher. Was my father's uncle doing the same?

Alarmed by this news, and sensing disaster, my father rushed off to Kessorepur. He somehow managed to convince his uncle once again to perform his duties till a new naikay could be found.

But a few months later, we heard something even worse—the majhi had started cutting down the trees in the village and was planning to cut down trees in the jaher, too. He started with a magnificent jamun that stood just outside our house in the village and cast a deep shade over our family well. The well, which had been dug under the supervision of my father's grandfather, provided water to nearly a third of our village. Of all the evil that my grandfather's brother committed, this hurt me the most. The cool water from the well, the cool shade of the jamun tree, its large, tart fruit, what a combination they had made.

The cutting down of the tree was a matter of

great hurt and humiliation for my father, too. Yet he let it pass. He did not want to spoil relations within the family. But, engrossed with politics, office and our family in Ghatsila, and struggling with his own anger and grief, he had lost track of events in the village and did not realize that they had set the majhi family, and Kessorepur, once again on the path to ruin. Once Dadu, the patriarch, had become ineffective with age, one of my father's half-sisters had got a paper signed by a local authority that only the children of my grandfather's second wife would have claim on our collective farmlands. This way, they were trying to grab all the property themselves.

As soon as he found out, my father filed a case and the court imposed a stay on the land. Land that had stayed together through generations, through war, Independence, the formation of a separate state, now stands disputed and divided. The majhi, Dadu's younger brother, we also found out, had sided with my father's half-siblings. Maybe that was what he hoped for, a share in the land, maybe that was why he stopped worshipping at the jaher. We could only guess, and tell each other that Simabonga had our village once more in its grip.

Even as the case dragged on in court, the majhi kept cutting down the trees in Kessorepur, as if to spite my father and his siblings. He felled an old, gnarled frangipani, then a jujube tree that gave the best fruit for miles around. Worst of all, he had the two huge sal trees in the jaher cut down, one after the other. What would he have gained by cutting down these trees? To kill a tree is savage. It is like murdering a man. Yet we couldn't say anything. Those trees were common property.

With the land falling into dispute, the ancestral house was also divided among the children of the two grandmothers. My father turned our side of the house into a concrete one. There was a huge star fruit tree in the courtyard. Everyone advised my father to have that tree cut down as it was causing hindrance to the way the new house was being built. My father, his life now intertwined with those of trees, refused to cut down that star fruit tree or even trim its branches. He left the tree as it was and built the house around it. The tree still casts its huge shadow on our courtyard. And the sight of its fruits in season, green when unripe, and yellow when ripe, strewn over the concrete floor is a sight to behold.

The jaher is now a jungle once more, overrun with bushes and grass, and a haunted emptiness marks the spot where the sal trees used to be.

~

My medical studies in Jamshedpur consumed me completely. Studies and the freedom to explore myself, my desires, my sexuality, and love, in ways which had never been possible earlier. I kept in touch with my parents, always carefully discussing only my studies and what was happening at home or in the village. I would be given the news from Kessorepur—the majhi had cut down one more tree, a couple of my half-uncles had almost come to blows over who would keep the fish from the ponds, someone or the other had died, the next court date for the hearing about the land had been announced. In between all this, my father retired, though they continued living in my mother's quarters on the factory premises. He now had all the time to devote to his garden. And each time I visited home, the garden would seem greener. Each time, a new sapling would have been planted, as though my father wanted to replace every tree that was cut down in Kessorepur. He would bring us the fruits of the season: mangoes, guavas, bananas, cashews. When we told him how big the bananas had grown or how delicious the mangoes tasted, I could see a rare joy and satisfaction in his eyes. He would return to his garden the next day and work doubly hard.

My mother retired a little before I left Jamshedpur. I went home to help them pack up a lifetime of memories and struggles and shift to our own house.

While I was in my housemanship year at the medical college, my father recommended that I appear for the Department of Health exams. I sat for the exams and passed them. There was nothing to keep me in Jamshedpur anymore, except for my doomed relationship with Samir. I went home to Ghatsila and soon received a posting at the Sadar hospital in Pakur, a small town with few friends.

Once I joined work, visits became rarer. Yet, on each trip home, I found my father working unrelentingly in his garden. And under his loving care, it flourished more than ever. A hibiscus tree, which had been falling over on one visit, would be propped up with bamboo staves on the next, covered with pale orange blossoms. The lime and lemon bushes would hang heavy with fruit in season. As would the mangoes, guavas, bananas and jackfruits. Before we left our quarters, my father had carefully plucked a litchi sapling from the premises as a memento. That, too, was flourishing. And just behind our kitchen, my mother and aunt cultivated their own little patch of earth. Thick, deep green vines of pui leaves climbed the iron grille of the verandah outside our kitchen. Tulsi, dhania and pudina grew lush in the cool space near the tubewell where the water keeps the earth always moist. Birds made their home in our garden. The caw-caws and the chee-chees would start at dawn and wake us up. At dusk, their raucous homecoming would tell us that the day was at an end.

~

Then, one night lonely in Pakur, the memories of Samir, the thoughts that he had forgotten me, that he wanted to forget me and block me out of his life forever, that he was someone else's, that he could never, ever be only mine, grew too much to bear. I ran a knife over my wrist. The wound wasn't deep and I woke up the next morning. The realization of what I had done, of what I was capable of doing to myself, frightened me and I took the next train home. My parents met me at the railway station, took in the bandages on my wrist, and said nothing. Once we got home, I went to my room and kept my stuff away.

My room is at the top of our house. It has a single bed, one open bookshelf, four bookshelves with doors, and an almirah. A fan hangs from the ceiling. From my bed, I can look out of the window into the verandah, beyond which I can see the broad-leaved sagwan that grows tall outside. It has always seemed to me a happy, cheerful creature. If I walked out to the verandah, I could reach out and touch its bark, its leaves. If I leaned my elbows on the parapet and looked down, I could see its clumps of golden flowers peek into my parents' room. The koels and ramchirayas which hopped on its branches seemed happy too. On some days, it seemed as if the sagwan was imploring us humans, the inhabitants of the house, to participate in its happiness, in the sheer joy of feeling the wind blow through its broad canopy, the rain tickling its bark in an intimate caress. I would feel that it was a foolish hope on its part.

On many afternoons, after lunch, I would lie in my bed looking out at the sagwan. A sparrow would fly in through the open window. As soon as she did,

I would quietly switch off the fan. She would always be unsure about her way inside. Perched on minute on the windowsill, she would fly to the top of one of the bookshelves, then onto the handle of another one. It seemed to me as if she was examining the books in my collection. On some days, I couldn't stand her scrutiny of my reading choices and shoo her out. On others, the heat would get too much and I would have to chase her away to switch on the fan.

After lunch, my father would go off into their room and I into mine. One day, he kept sitting at the dining table.

Then he said, abruptly, 'You know, we have our own alarm clock now.'

I didn't know what to make of that and said, 'Thik hai.'

'Haan,' he replied.

My mother joined us at the table, having finished putting away the lunch dishes. My father then began his story.

All the windows of their bedroom have mercury

glass panes to keep the glare of the sun out. Every morning for the last several days, too early to get up and too late to go back to sleep, they were being woken up by a knock on the window-pane. Assuming that it must be a branch that was hitting the window, my father said to my mother that he would trim it soon. This continued for several days until, one day, something unusual happened. The knocking began, a two-beat knock at intervals, then stopped for several minutes, then began again, and wouldn't stop.

My mother went outside the house to investigate. She found a large, long-tailed drongo perched on the grill, looking intently at its reflection in the silver-coated glass and quarrelling with it. It would peck at it, fly away, and as if it remembered its frustration, come flying back to perch on the grill once more.

The three of us had a good laugh. The first, it felt, after a long time.

I asked my father, 'Papa, can we grow a sal tree in our garden?' Surprisingly, we don't have a single sal tree.

My father laughed, and said, 'Sal tree needs a lot of time, beta. And a lot of care. It needs a certain type of soil. Red soil. Of the kind that is found in our jaher. On this soil here, sal wouldn't grow that well unless it is well looked after. And I don't have much energy and patience left any more to care for sal saplings. '

It is true, my father does not have much energy and patience left. He doesn't harbour any ambitions, he doesn't involve himself in party work, and only goes out now and then to meet a few of his old friends. He attends the court hearings regularly, but increasingly with a sense of resignation.

And when he tells me that sal trees grow well in jahers, then remembers the trees of his youth, which his uncle cut down mercilessly, I can sense his sorrow. Not only about the trees but about everything: his life in politics, the downfall of Kessorepur and, I can't help but think, about me—a grown man, a doctor, sitting at home, nursing a wound and a broken heart, incapable of sharing anything with his parents.

I once read somewhere that the single-minded pursuit of one course over a lifetime can only be justified if one engages in two enterprises—building a garden, or raising a child. I now understand that my father's garden is truly his child. And this child gives him the happiness and peace of mind that nothing else could ever give him.

CPSIA information can be obtained
at www.ICGtesting.com
Printed in the USA
BVHW061221100221
599730BV00006B/1559

9 789388 326858